gambling with fire

gambling
with
fire

david
montrose

Introduction by
John McFetridge

A
Ricochet
Book

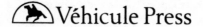
Véhicule Press

Published with the assistance of the Canada Council for the Arts, the Canada Book Fund of the Department of Canadian Heritage, and the Société de développement des entreprises culturelles du Québec (SODEC).

Funded by the Government of Canada
Financé par le gouvernement du Canada

Canadä

Series editor: Brian Busby
Adaptation of original cover: J.W. Stewart
Special assistance: Diane Carlson and Alexander Keys
Typeset in Minion by Simon Garamond
Printed by Marquis Printing Inc.

Originally published in 1968
Original copyright © 1968, this edition 2016

LIBRARY AND ARCHIVES CANADA
CATALOGUING IN PUBLICATION

Montrose, David, 1920-1968, author
Gambling with fire / David Montrose;
introduction by John McFetridge.

(Ricochet books)
Originally published: Don Mills, Ontario: Longmans Canada, 1969.
Issued in print and electronic formats.
ISBN 978-1-55065-441-7 (paperback).– ISBN 978-1-55065-447-9 (epub)

I. McFetridge, John, 1959-, writer of introduction
II. Title. III. Series:
Ricochet books

PS8526.O593G36 2016   C813'.54   C2015-907353-7
C2015-907354-5

Published by Véhicule Press, Montréal, Québec, Canada
www.vehiculepress.com

Distribution in Canada by LitDistCo
www.litdistco.ca

Distributed in the U.S. by Independent Publishers Group
www.ipgbook.com

Printed in Canada on FSC® certified paper

MIX
Paper from responsible sources
FSC® C103567

To my most compassionate friend,
Lev Chipman

INTRODUCTION

John McFetridge

CRIME FICTION WRITERS are often associated with a particular city; Chandler's L.A., Hammett's San Francisco, Rankin's Edinburgh, Parker's Boston. David Montrose wrote three private-eye novels set in Montreal, but it's really with this book that he gets to the soul of the city. This at first seems a little strange because the narrator of those P.I. novels is born-and-bred Montrealer Russell Teed while *Gambling with Fire* is seen through the eyes of recently arrived European immigrant Franz Loebek.

But it works.

Gambling with Fire was first published in 1969. Although nowhere in the book does it say which year the events take place, it's certainly early in the post-war years, when Montreal was still an open city; it's pre-Drapeau and Pax Plante, pre-Quiet Revolution, pre-Expo. My hunch is that this book was written before Montrose's P.I. novels: *The Crime on Cote des Neiges* (1951), *Murder Over Dorval* (1952), and *The Body on Mount Royal* (1953). Maybe he had trouble finding a publisher for this book and put aside his aristocratic character in favour of a more streetwise private eye. Maybe an agent or a publisher suggested a non-immigrant character. Agents and publishers make all kinds of suggestions. Even today most Canadian crime writers have a story of someone in the business suggesting they set their books in a country other than Canada.

I have no idea if the suggestion of moving the action out of Montreal ever came up in those days, but I'm very glad that Montrose chose to write about the city he knew so well. When one of Loebek's English friends says

Montreal is a small town, Loebek says, "It is a city of over two million persons."

His friend explains:

> Of whom one-third are English. Of which part, perhaps one-thousandth are the controllers of the industry, the business, the financial houses, the banks. That means there are three hundred men to meet. You can see most of them a dozen times over in a few months... Montreal society is the most fluid in the world. You need only a certain amount of money, or the appearance of it, and a ready capacity for enjoyment and entertaining, to enter.

Of course, that a small number of people control business, financial houses, and the banks was probably the same everywhere, but Montrose puts the situation to good work in this novel. Russell Teed's whole world was pretty much just the one-third of the city that was English, and even then mostly among the one-thousandth of the population in Westmount. In *Gambling with Fire*, Montrose takes his knowledge of the one-(thousandth) percenters and mixes them with the criminal underworld. Using the displaced European aristocrat Franz Loebek is a terrific choice to bridge the gap.

Loebek himself is in between. He even realizes it: "I am on the Côte des Neiges, the pass between the two hills. I am neither on the one nor the other."

If *Gambling with Fire* was written in the years just after the war, it's likely Montrose was influenced and inspired by Hugh MacLennan's 1945 novel *Two Solitudes*, and maybe also by the series of 1949 *Le Devoir* articles by journalist Gérard Filion and lawyer Pacifique Plante exposing organized crime and police corruption in Montreal.

Diving into the two solitudes, Montrose has Loebek fall for a married woman, Nicole, who won't even consider a divorce because the Catholic Church won't allow it. Nicole is a product of both solitudes, as Montrose explains, "It's quite the fashion here for English families to have their children learn French by having a French-Canadian nurse-maid. The Desmarais family did it in reverse. Nicole went to English schools."

Nicole herself says to Loebek:

> "Oh, come! You are European. You know what is traditional and accepted as the procedure for a respectable girl, everywhere but on the North American continent. She must be concerned not primarily with love, but with marriage to a man of whom her parents approve. If he is physically attractive, if love can be developed, all to the good. But in the absence of love there is the marriage, the approval of the parents, security, care, a good home…"

"And this is true everywhere except on this continent."

"You should realize that French Canada is more a part of Europe, in many ways, than of North America."

"Yet exposed to both influences."

"Yes, and I more than most people of my race. You know something of my life? My father was wealthy, and enough of a realist to believe the English would always be the powerful race in this country. Our home life was traditional French-Canadian, but we lived in Westmount; all of our friends were English. They were English Catholics, preferably, but many were not even of our own religion. We had few French friends. Our schooling was in English."

"Yet your ideas—for instance, your idea of marriage—remained typically French?"

"There was my mother."

Montrose goes a little further into the cultural divers-ity of Montreal with the character of Linda, who tells Loebek, "I'm not one of your svelte, frightened, purebred Anglo-Saxon beauties from a tired old Westmount family. I'm a slum kid." And not even an Irish slum kid.

And, as *Gambling with Fire* is, after all, a crime novel, Loebek quickly gets involved with the Montreal under-world. When he does, his European sophistication is a pretty good fit. Approached about a business deal, Loebek says, "Is it legal?"

And he isn't surprised at all by the response, "It is tolerated."

Loebek describes himself as "an uprooted man. I am a humbled aristocrat. And since I am no longer able to work at my profession of being a landed gentleman, I am lost... I am not a man of enterprise. Therefore, I do not belong, I do not fit into this society. If North America becomes the pattern for the rest of the world—as sometimes seems horribly likely—I will not even fit into this century."

I think you can make the argument that Montrose was right and North America did become the pattern for the rest of the world.

The business deal introduces Loebek to the French-Canadian underworld boss, Rosaire Beaumage, a kind of early version of suburb-living Tony Soprano, holed up in his large Outremont home. It may be on the other side of the mountain, but it's still on the mountain.

And Montrose is very good at showing the similarities between the business world and the criminal world. For example, this exchange could be in a boardroom or a backroom:

> "You've no idea of right or wrong—"
> "Neither have you, you old pirate. Just what's legal and illegal."
> "—Or of what's wise and what's unwise."

In some ways *Gambling with Fire* was ahead of its time, even when finally published in 1969. It's a crime novel but not a murder mystery. Oh, people get murdered, but there's no mystery, no real investigation. The main character isn't a cop or a private eye or even an amateur sleuth. Like Franz Loebek being between the mountains, or between the business world and the criminal world, or between the two solitudes of Montreal, the novel is in between.

For years I heard exactly the same thing about my own novels while trying to find a publisher; not literary enough to be literature and not hard-boiled enough to be a mystery.

Even Montrose seemed to know that he was writing something that wasn't quite this or that, and has one character say, "Take detective stories. Try to keep the reader from solvin' the plot. What if you can't solve it yourself?"

Today, *Gambling with Fire* would be simply be called a crime novel and take its place on the shelves beside other novels that are not mystery series and don't have detectives or private eyes as the main character—novels like George V. Higgins' *The Friends of Eddie Coyle* and those of Elmore Leonard. In the fifties, as in 1969, *Gambling with Fire* fell between the cracks and disappeared.

The bad news is that there is only one Franz Loebek novel. The good news is it's back in print.

John McFetridge was born and raised in Montreal. He is the author of six novels. His Constable Eddie Dougherty series, *Black Rock* (2014) and *A Little More Free* (2015), are set in Montreal. He lives in Toronto.

ONE

Scene One

A MAN WHO HAD BEEN an aristocrat, and then a hero, and was now nothing, sat in the bar room of a small Montreal hotel in the early September afternoon. His hand held a drained glass. He twirled the glass and watched it, idly, and in it saw a symbol of his future; empty, useless, cold.

His name was Franz Loebek. The surname was thought to be a corruption of Loebener, and had once been preceded by the aristocratic *von*. The name had changed, but neither the feeling nor the possessions of aristocracy had altered, when his family ceased being lords of the Austrian Empire and became landowners of Czechoslovakia. Nominally, he was a Czech. But he did not even speak the Czech tongue; his language was German, his heritage Holy Roman Empire, his country Austria.

The muted yellow sunlight cut through Venetian blinds and ran in a beam to his feet, finding wild colours in the worn heavy carpet. The bar room, in early afternoon, was like a score of the other hotel bars in Montreal; cool, quiet, dim, with a few solitary and relaxed drinkers, a sense of suspended time.

Opposite him at the little table sat an utterly bald, bespectacled older man. Franz almost listened as he talked with an inbred volubility—the voice easy, gestures slow…

Clack. Clack-clack.

The woman had stepped into the bar through one of the narrow little swinging doors, releasing it with a quick push. It oscillated sharply to rest behind her, the noise raucous in the silence of the bar. The drinkers looked up; and it had been her intention to draw their notice, for she surveyed them one by one as they stared.

Franz Loebek glanced up, and felt his glance held and turned to a gaze. She had a perfect rounded face, the skin dark and yet translucent, and smooth so that a highlight of reflection caught at her cheek. Her eyes, dark as well, were set wide and deep in the structure of her face. She had black and plentiful hair that a bounty of natural oils made shining and smooth in its undulating descent to her shoulders; her eyebrows, the same black, had not been plucked and gave, from the distance, a focus to her face.

She could be twenty, thirty. If twenty, she had been trained in a svelte school of fashion and society; if thirty, she was nearly ageless, still fresh with the firm, clean flesh that seldom lasts long past adolescence. For her body was formed as an artist might sketch freehand—each line placed, in a kind of easy spontaneity, precisely true.

It was a body, he thought, seeing her stand with the black fur coat over her shoulders, hands clasped at her waist, in a sheath-tight dress, a body that deserved to go proudly free in the warmth on some deserted shore.

Franz saw her in his mind nude, unashamed, and saw her dressed again. And thought he would not forget her. And suddenly said to himself, very deeply in his mind: I have not thought that of a woman before. Not in all these years.

She met his gaze an instant, and her eyes passed directly on. She turned and left the room.

Loebek thrust her from his thought. Morris Winter was asking a question:

"Why did you come to Canada?"

"I was permitted to. There was nowhere else to go except back. And there was nothing left behind me."

"After the war, in exchange for five years of fighting, a fresh start. That is better than the war did for some."

"I suppose so." It was doubtful whether a fresh start was a good or a bad thing, and one could not argue about it. It was simply too soon to tell.

Winter said, "What can I do for you? Have you other friends in the city? Have you enough money? I am back at my old work, and it is prosperous now."

"Thanks, my friend. I have money."

It had been a mistake to call Winter, he thought. He wanted only a little companionship, and Winter thought he wanted help.

"Will you stay in Montreal?"

"Yes," Franz said. "I have been here alone for two days, trying to get the feeling of this city. I have it. It is a complete city, a real city—can I say what I mean? There is a variety and a true, unique life here, like the cities of Europe. The old parts are like Paris, even sometimes like my own Vienna. The new parts are better than European cities."

He looked around again at the bar. It was small, very restrained. Like some of the small bars in London. Deep seats and heavy old carpeting. Lamps with dark shades and small bulbs; no glare, no sharp lights and shadows. The waiters were slim, straight and correct; they moved easily and silently over the padded floor, efficient but unhurried. There was a pleasant air of calm.

"A complete city," Franz Loebek repeated. "You can see it built up, tier on tier, looking from the top of Mount Royal. You see the shipping of the river, the factories and warehouses, the financial streets, the shopping streets, the university and the hospitals. It is a neat city. The river is its perimeter and it rises, circle on concentric circle, to the mountaintop."

"There is also a second mountain."

"That destroys none of the symmetry. The city rises also in layers to the top of Westmount, but this is a more particular aspect of the city. The poorest live at the riverbank, the richest homes are near the peak of Westmount mountain."

"And what will you do? How will you fit into these neat circles of working and living?"

Franz shrugged. "I have not decided. What does a refugee do? Perhaps I could be *maître d'hôtel* at some small restaurant. Perhaps a store clerk."

"What did you do before the war?"

"Nothing."

"Literally—nothing?"

"I managed my father's estate. That was nothing. I hunted and rode, I was an expert guide to Vienna. I was an enthusiastic pilot. But I am used up as a flier, I will not go on with that."

Winter said without hesitancy, "I would be happy to have you work for me. You could be a croupier—no, a cashier. I have need always of honest cashiers. And there would be no undesirable person in authority over you. You would report directly to me alone. I own my own club, as much as such a thing can be owned."

"My thanks. I will think about it."

"Why do you not say yes?"

"Squeamishness, perhaps. This country is taking me in when I have nowhere to go. Should I aid in breaking her laws?"

"My friend, laws against gambling are made to be broken. They cannot hold where there is wealth and a love of excitement. They are made by fools—"

"To protect fools."

"But we take no money from fools who are poor. No one who cannot afford to pay well, without feeling the loss, is knowingly permitted in the house. The wheels and dice are honest; some win, some lose. The house percentage is fair. This is an ethical business, Franz."

He said again, "Thanks. I'll remember your offer."

"It is almost a respectable business. It is open quite freely to all, with the permission of one man—an evil creature named Beaumage. But we pay him and he leaves us alone; so do the police. You would enjoy it."

"I may come to you later," Loebek said. "I know how to reach you."

"I would be honoured to have you work for me. I admired you very much, during the war. You never found your plane less than perfect?"

"Its performance was always superb."

"I assigned the best mechanic to it. And always, just before you flew, I checked it myself. I owed you that service. With a perfect plane, you had something to match your own skill."

Loebek smiled; he inclined his head. "Thank you, Sergeant."

The waiter took the empty glasses from their table and set down two fresh drinks. Winter raised his glass.

"Your health, Squadron-Leader."

"Former Squadron-Leader."

Winter said uneasily, "I can understand that you might not wish to work for me. It seems unfair. Everything is upside down since the war."

"No, no. Why should I not work for you? I am displaced. It has yet to be established where I will fit into this country. Just now I feel entirely useless. Probably I should be shining your shoes."

Winter could think of no way to treat this remark except as a great joke, and laughed heartily. Then he went on, "Some other members of the Squadron are here in Montreal. There are powerful men—powerful families— among them. You will talk to them."

"No, I will talk to no one else. I will begin to see them when I am settled."

Winter drew a thin morocco case from his coat. "When that time comes, please visit me," he asked. He selected a card and handed it to Franz. "I hope you may enjoy an evening at my club."

"I shall come," Franz promised. After Winter left he sat for some time, sipping his Scotch and water very slowly. At intervals, taking cigarettes and a small gold lighter from his pocket, he lit up and smoked. Slowly he was becoming accustomed to Canadian cigarettes; they were packed closely with mild golden tobacco, slow-burning and of a rather delicate flavor. Who would expect Canadians to smoke a connoisseur's cigarette?

By that thought he was judging Canadians. Yet what did he really know of them? The men who had fought with him had been accurate, careless killers in the air; rough, hard drinkers in the mess. The few times he had considered them, he had placed them somewhere between Australians and Americans: a type of mechanically gifted frontiersmen. And now—he was not sure.

Here was this great city of Montreal, old and seeming as educated in vice as European cities; berthed in her docks, ships of the world. Bars like London, churches like Paris, narrow streets that could be Marseilles, neon streets that could be New York.

I must find the pattern, he thought. I must overcome this sense of being displaced. I travelled quietly along, was thrust suddenly into a stream of action, and now have reached the far bank. I need only find the pattern and fit myself into it.

He drained his glass and pushed back the chair. As he came to the doorway, the girl with black hair entered the bar again. This time she made no unnecessary noise, but anger showed in her face.

"Good afternoon, Mrs. Porter-Smythe." One of the silent attendants had approached, and addressed her.

"Alex, have you seen Mr. Porter-Smythe?" she asked abruptly.

"No, madam."

"I expected to meet him here."

"If you'd care to take a table in the alcove, I'll—"

"No. Thank you, Alex."

She turned sharply and collided with Franz, who had been unable to move past her to the door.

"Oh! *Pardon.*"

"*Celà ne fait rien, madame.*"

She looked up to his face, curiously. A French-Canadian would have said, "*C'est rien*," and with a different intonation. In French she asked, "You are from France, m'sieur?"

"No. Czechoslovakia."

There was something in his face that made her want to continue the conversation. He was a tall, lean man with dark blond hair cut very short; with a fair, untanned skin. His forehead was broad, his cheek-bones high and well-defined with the straight cheeks, neither full nor hollowed, falling to a firm mouth and cleanly-squared chin.

He had the look of far space in his eyes.

Franz Loebek smiled. He bowed to her, not with heel-clicking stiffness but with the ease of custom handed down from another time.

He walked slowly out into the brown September dusk.

Scene Two

"Squadron-Leader Loebek!"

Franz kept his face expressionless, but felt extreme annoyance. He had no wish to be recognized, and had been very lucky; in three months of living in Montreal, this was the first person to call him by name.

The man, in evening dress, at first looked unfamiliar. He was gay from drink, and saluted lop-sidedly to his forehead. Then Franz remembered. His name was Gladwin, and he had been a navigator in the squadron toward the end of the war.

"Darling, this is an occasion!" Gladwin led forward the girl he was escorting. "May I present Franz Loebek, the Czech ace. He was Squadron-Leader of number ten—my operational unit overseas. Franz, Linda Warren."

Loebek bowed and gave his set smile. "Good evening,

Miss Warren. Good evening, sir. Two?"

"Please," the girl said. She had an arrogant face, long and strong-featured, and lustrous long blonde hair. She radiated an insolent, dominating vitality, an air of uncivilized force. She was attractive rather than beautiful, but she compelled attention.

Franz looked at her an instant too long for her liking and she said impatiently, "Yes, a table for two."

He led them to a table. As he returned to his post at the door Gladwin was saying, too loud not to overhear, "Well, that's a hell of a note. Head-waiter! He was my Squadron-Leader. After what he did for this country, you'd think—"

"He seems a fairly good head-waiter," Linda said.

Franz repressed a smile. I'll take it as a compliment, he thought. I want to be a good head-waiter.

For this was how he had fitted in; this was his place in the Montreal pattern. The dining-room of the Chatham Hotel was small—though it served excellent food to its discriminating habitués—and there was no great prestige to his job. It paid enough to rent a small, clean room in an old house on Sherbrooke Street, and to buy cigarettes and drinks and minor articles of clothing. The Chatham provided his well-fitting dress suit, and his meals. The work was pleasant.

It was a late hour, even for fashionable diners, and he was not busy. He found it difficult to keep his eyes from the girl. She had a big-boned, almost angular face, with shoulders as wide as her hips; yet the womanly roundness of her form, built upon such an unpromising base, was truly voluptuous. Because of her strength and solidity, as much as her deep breasts and smooth thighs, she appeared a woman of great sexuality.

He compared her with the dark girl he had seen months ago in the bar of this same hotel. That woman, whom he knew only as Mrs. Porter-Smythe, had been the only one to leave a lasting memory since his arrival in Montreal.

There had been others—a beautiful young prostitute who might have come home to his room had she not distressed him with a unique brand of North American super-salesmanship; a woman who always wore black, and sat eternally alone in a bar he often visited—who left passing impressions. But Mrs. Porter-Smythe was the only one he hoped to see again.

Linda Warren looked up once, and met his gaze fully, and seemed to take satisfaction from the fact that he was watching her.

He had an odd feeling that she wanted to fight with him, to test his will. The unspoken challenge brought an answer. He tingled at the thought of how stimulating, how testing she would be to conquer; how fiery in surrender. He felt she could give a man, in a night, an unmatchable experience. And she would be harder to live with than the very flames of hell.

After dinner, as the couple came out, Gladwin was less drunken; the meal had cleared his head. He smiled at Franz, and nodded; Franz bowed. Linda Warren went toward the ladies' room, and Gladwin got his coat quickly from the checker and came back to the dining-room, tangling a white silk scarf about his neck.

"You remember me, Franz?"

"Yes, Mr. Gladwin."

"The name is Bill."

"Yes, sir. You understand my position."

"I understand no damn' position at all. What are you doing here? Is this the best the government did for you?"

"The government let me come to Canada, and afterward I was left on my own. That was exactly what I wanted."

"Could we get together for a talk? Come and see me, will you?"

"Thank you, sir. I will."

"No, damn you, you wouldn't. Where are you living?"

"On Sherbrooke west, near here."

"I'll come to see you. What times are you there?"

"After midnight I am usually in my room. The house number is nine-ninety. Knock on the window just to the left of the front door."

"I'll come late tonight," Gladwin said.

Linda Warren returned to claim him.

"I had an excellent dinner, Squadron-Leader."

"I'm glad, Miss Warren."

"Weren't you a Count in Czechoslovakia?"

"No. The second son of a Baron."

She laughed. "Even without the war, you'd have been sent off to seek your fortune."

"Even without the war," he agreed, smiling.

"And being a head-waiter here is better than going back to the aristocratic life in Czechoslovakia?"

"There is little aristocratic life left there."

"Oh. Then I expect you appreciate living here."

A party of four came to the door, and Franz was able to return to his duties. When he came back they had gone.

Carl, the young waiter whose station was near the door, said, "Those aren't the two richest youngsters in Montreal. But it is nice to have them notice you."

"Yes?"

"The Warren girl's a brat."

"She seems a spoiled little bitch. She took pleasure in being rude to me, because she did not like the way I looked at her when she came in. I think she senses I am not afraid of her."

"You are probably the only unafraid man in her last decade of experience. She is an exquisite woman, but the very look of her is arrogant. Not at all like a Canadian woman, but like a princess of somewhere in Europe. She knows men will crawl at her feet, and despises them for it. She knows there is nothing she wants that someone will not bring her."

"You know much about her."

"When I was a waiter at the St. Mark Club, I served

her father. It might have been predicted his daughter would be such a woman. Warren is an Englishman who made success in big business. Have you known the type? Cold as iced vichyssoise. They have that British reserve, combined with a strong acquisitive instinct and the innate conviction they were born to control men. Beside them American tycoons are boisterous little children."

"So. She inherits his temperament."

"I think it is more than that. They say, with all his cold dominant will, she can twist him instantly to her wishes. After such an accident of birth, it is no surprise she finds other men small game."

"She should be beaten black and blue. I wonder whether it is too late?"

But much more satisfying than a contest of wills with Linda, he thought suddenly, would be a new meeting with the Porter-Smythe woman. There, though, he was decidedly too late.

Scene Three

The room was the size of a large closet. A single bed, one chair, a wash basin, a high, cheap painted box for a wardrobe. Franz came in very tired at midnight. The tap on his window came at one o'clock. He went to the front door and led Bill Gladwin back to his room.

"Drink?" he asked. "I have some rye here. No ice, but the tap water is cold."

"Thanks, a small one. Franz, I'm being presumptuous forcing myself on you."

"I am always glad to see someone from the Squadron."

"I have a small speech to spout. It will probably make you angry. Then you can throw me out."

"I will not do that, of course. But"—he searched his memory for the man's first name—"but, Bill, it will do no good if you try to offer me a job, a loan, your influence. I am a refugee. I want to stand alone, and I am doing so. I am quite well qualified to be a head-waiter, but aside from that I am useless—a specimen of decadent aristocracy. I will not have you foist me upon your friends. I will not be put in a false position."

"Listen for two minutes," Gladwin said. "I'll tell you what you must do. Quit your job at the Chatham immediately, before anyone else sees you there. After that, get out of this place. Go to the Frontenac Apartments. They'll tell you they have a waiting list, but if you mention my name they'll forget about that. Take a suite big enough for entertaining, and then call me."

"And what would I use to pay the rent?"

"They don't ask for advance deposits at the Frontenac. By the time your rent is due, you'll have a job that will pay it ten times over."

"No. Thank you, no."

"Why not?"

"The idea is ridiculous. You propose that your friends will offer me a place. But these are friends you have known, here in Montreal, all your life. Do you think they would accept me overnight?"

"Of course they would. You don't understand Montreal, Franz. If you meet just a few of the right people, in the right circumstances, nothing else matters. You see, this is an amazingly small town."

"It is a city of over two million persons."

"Of whom one-third are English. Of which part, perhaps one-thousandth are the controllers of the industry, the business, the financial houses, the banks. That means there are three hundred men to meet. You can see most of them a dozen times over in a few months. As for their not accepting you—that's nonsense. Montreal society is the most fluid in the world. You need only a certain amount of money, or the appearance of it, and a ready capacity for enjoyment and entertaining, to enter."

"Granted, then, I could enter your society. That does not guarantee me a job."

"If I were in anything but a law office, I'd give you a job myself. I'll make a bet with you. Two weeks after you get an apartment in the Frontenac, you'll have at least four good job offers."

"But—for what would you consider me fitted?"

"Business requires no special training and very few special aptitudes. You have to have a good background for an executive job. You must meet people easily, manage them without too much friction, be able to size up a situation and apply rudimentary logic to determine the action to be taken. You must have a small gift for reporting, verbally or on paper, a summary of a problem. That's all. You could fit in, in the space of weeks."

"The structure of North American business is strange to me," Franz protested. "You must remember I have lived a semi-feudal life. I would get myself completely lost in a day."

"Oh, no, you wouldn't. Why not give it a try?"

"You are my second Samaritan. I must answer the first."

"What did he suggest? Something specific?"

"He wished to make me cashier in a gambling club." Gladwin laughed. "And you refused?"

"I told him I would think it over."

"And what do you tell me?"

"That I will think your idea over, also."

"Then my offer is no better than the gambler's," Gladwin concluded, again amused.

"In one way it is much the same. It is asking me to play a part, act a role. As a gambler, I would be in an artificial position. So, also, as a business executive. Perhaps I am better off to stay where I am—only a host, and at that a paid host. But in my normal role."

Gladwin drained his glass and stood. "Let me know if you change your mind about that," he said.

"I will. Thank you for trying to help."

"Listen, Franz, I'm not trying to help you. You can help yourself. If you choose to do it in this way, I'm here to be made of use. That's all. I'd more gladly do something for you than do most of the favours my business calls for."

"Thank you again."

Franz said, "The girl, Miss Warren. She is interesting."

"Linda? You probably gathered she was a bit forceful."

"Dominant."

"She needs someone to manage her. I've about decided I have other problems."

"She seems too spoiled for any man. The instant she possesses one, I wager, she no longer desires him."

"Quite. She respects what she can't control, nothing else."

"Some day there will be a man too strong for her."

"He'd have to be quite a man. I wish him only one thing. I hope he won't marry her."

"No," Franz said. "I'm sure he wouldn't."

They went to the door. Franz suddenly remembered his curiosity about a dark girl. "Do you know some people named Porter-Smythe?" he asked Bill Gladwin.

"Oh, of course. Where did you run into them?"

"Not them, her. I encountered her quite by chance."

"Nicole. I'm not surprised you enquire. Isn't she lovely?"

"Yes," he said briefly.

"Nicole Desmarais. She was a funny, unsettled girl, sort of displaced. Her family is thoroughly French-Canadian, but exceedingly wealthy. They have a huge Westmount house. She was brought up there—with an English-speaking governess. It's quite the fashion here for English families to have their children learn French by having a French-Canadian nursemaid. The Desmarais family did it in reverse. Nicole went to English schools for some years, finally to a convent. Then she came out of the convent and married Porter-Smythe.

Shows you what convent life must be like."

"Who is he—Porter-Smythe?"

"Oh, small, quiet millions in an unimportant, lucrative little business. Screws, nuts and bolts, I think. Not Charles, of course—the one Nicole married. His father founded it. Charles just sits and tries to annoy the faithful employees who are holding the business together."

"I wondered who her husband was," Franz said slowly. "It doesn't really matter."

"Charles doesn't matter. That I guarantee. You want to meet them formally?"

"Charles can hardly matter as little as I would wish."

"He might. You want to meet them? Just do what I say. Take a Frontenac apartment. I'll bring them there the first time you entertain."

"I still will think it over."

Scene Four

"Charles! Charles Porter-Smythe!"

Charles turned. Linda Warren was slightly taller than he, and almost undoubtedly weighed more. She bore down upon him and seemed to overwhelm him, merely by linking her arm in his and bending toward him. Several people in the crowded hotel lobby, he saw with vain annoyance, were amused.

"Charles, I haven't seen you in weeks!"

"Why, no, my dear. Come into the Piccadilly and let me buy you a drink."

"Wouldn't think of taking you back in there. You just came out, I saw you. Been priming yourself for dinner?"

"Oh, yes. With some business friends."

"Then let's have dinner. Come on, I've a dozen things to tell you about."

"My dear, I wish I could. But I positively must get home. Nicole is expecting me. Dinner"—he looked at the Swiss master-work on his wrist—"is probably on the table now."

"Are you going to let your marriage ruin a friendship as old as ours?"

"Listen, you brat, you're being ridiculous. I've got to get home to dinner. That's that. Can I drive you somewhere? Or will you stay here and stalk the Mount Royal lobby until you find another man to pounce on?"

"Don't want another man," she said positively. "Want you, Charles. After all, those business friends could have kept you another hour, couldn't they?"

"If they had, or if you do, my marriage might dissolve."

"Not much of a marriage, then."

"Oh, I don't know," he said casually. "Maybe I haven't been treating it well enough."

"I can see you have things to tell me, too. Come on."

"And how many people will see us having dinner, and jam the telephone trying to tell Nicole?"

"We'll go somewhere very quiet. I don't want to have dinner here this evening. We'll go to the Chatham."

"Oh, fine. Somewhere quiet! Quietest place in town, all of my friends think so. Never meet more than a dozen of 'em when I go there."

"Well, I want you to take me to the Chatham. It's too early for anyone we know to be there, and besides, they always stop in the bar first. We'll go right into the dining-room."

Charles gave in. He let Linda lead him across the wide blue-walled lobby of the Mount Royal to the front entrance; he summoned his car, and drove to the Chatham.

As they came through the lobby of the Chatham toward the dining-room, Franz looked up and steeled himself for trouble. There was something unwholesome in the picture they presented: the big, rangy girl, the small rabbit-chinned man drawn along with her as though caught in the suction of her movement.

He recognized Linda Warren at once, as much by her walk and the carriage of her earthy body, as by the long dark face.

"Good evening, Miss Warren; Sir."

She regarded him cynically. "You don't know what it means to me to be recognized by head-waiters." Without actually touching Porter-Smythe, she gave the impression of dragging him into the conversation by his hand. "Charles, this is Squadron-Leader somebody. A great friend of Bill Gladwin's. He's the second son of a Baron."

"Eh?" said Porter-Smythe. "Oh." He nodded.

Franz felt his ears redden. He thought of horse-whips. He thought of the way the servant girls had been pulled by their hair into the cellars, to be beaten, when they misbehaved, back on his father's estate.

"I'd rather like the table by the second window. You'll give us that one, won't you, Squadron-Leader?"

Franz bowed. He prided himself that the cold smile he managed was unaffected by his feelings. "Certainly, Miss Warren."

He left them at their table, bowing again, and returned to the doorway. The waiter Carl stood at his station, flushed and staring rigidly ahead of him. He had overheard.

"Bitch," said Franz dispassionately.

Carl nodded.

"There are some drawbacks to this position," Franz said thoughtfully, "that one could hardly have foreseen."

TWO

Scene One

THE DOOR OF THE HOSPITAL room was open, but Franz paused before he went in. Winter was cranked halfway up in the high bed. He looked white and wizened. His bald skull and beaky nose shone in the harsh, sterile light making him seem more bird than man. His voice had weakened.

"Come in, come in," he called to Franz.

"I only heard by chance that you were here. I wish I had known before."

"I'm not here for long. Only the rest of my life."

"Nonsense."

"Oh, it will not be today. Nor tomorrow. Perhaps a week. Stomach cancer. A little indigestion, you think, Omigod, have I ulcers? You go to a doctor and he sends you here. They cut you open and shake their heads and sew you up again. I cannot complain. I am full of some drug. No pain at all."

Franz sat down beside the bed and waited. He could think of nothing to say.

"I did most things I wanted to," Winter went on. "Except get married and raise four or five children, but it did not look as though I would do that anyway. I did not start at it in time. The war came along when I was just thinking of settling down. I couldn't stay out. I volunteered," he said proudly. "You did not know that, did you?"

"No, I did not realize that."

"I always wanted to be around when things happened. Well, I was there to see the world crack up. You believe that? When the war started, it was going to bring forth a brand new world after it had been won. Before it was half over any fool could see how wrong that was. The war was only the beginning of things. I have read enough history to believe that all civilizations crack up in the end."

"I suppose so, in a sense."

"Well, it's your turn now. All you living bastards. I'm not as sorry about those children as I might have been."

"The doctors have told you their diagnosis? You are not trying to worry yourself to death?"

"It took one day to persuade them I could take it. They told me."

"Is there anything I can do for you, my friend? Anyone I can tell, or bring to see you?"

"No. No one in this city. There are two things you can do."

"Of course."

"There is a man named Willie Cameron. My head croupier at the club. I had to fire him, and I have an idea he is in the city with nothing to do. If you can trace him, I want to give him money for train fare, to get away. And a few hundred dollars; he is undoubtedly without a cent by now. I'll give you a cheque for him."

"I'll find him."

"The second thing: I would like an Air Force funeral. Could you see to it?"

"Yes, when it is time to think of that."

"A funeral with muffled drums, the flag over me, the band playing the Dead March. The boys slow-marching. Have you ever seen anything more restrained than those funerals, Franz? The cymbals crash, and are muffled, and crash again. The drums roll slowly, and then all the brass in the band comes in, low and sad on a minor key. It's slow and sorrowful, but it has much beauty. The only beautiful funeral in the world, Franz. I think I earned that. Most of the things I have done have been wrong, or selfish, or just foolish. But I gave all I could to the Air Force. That is the only thing I want remembered when they bury me."

The long speech was too much for him and his paleness had shaded from white almost to grey as his voice went on, more and more weakly.

"Crank me down, Franz."

Loebek lowered the mattress slowly and gently, letting the crank creep smoothly in his fingers.

"I want to rest now, Franz. Come to see me tomorrow, I have something more I must tell you. Now I am too tired, but I will rest and become a little stronger."

Franz backed away from the pallid man, out of the white room. Morrie Winter had closed his eyes.

A man in a white suit stood in the corridor, holding a stethoscope carelessly in one hand. He was young, very cleanly scrubbed, and his dark hair was cropped short enough to reveal all the bumps and hollows of his broad skull.

"I beg your pardon," he said. "I'm Doctor Wallace. Might I speak to you for a minute?"

"I should very much like to talk with you; I should like to ask about Mr. Winter's chance for—"

Wallace interrupted briskly: "Could we step this way?"

He led the way to a broad sun-room at the end of the corridor, a place walled with glass, floored with dull red tile, furnished with wicker chairs and great ferns. The windows looked on one side back to the glistening snow and black-limbed trees of the upper slopes of Mount Royal, on the other side down upon the heart of the city.

A man rose as they entered the room. He was a big, heavy man, a little soft but with a flat belly and erect shoulders. The blue serge suit he wore was old enough to shine at the elbows; it needed pressing.

The intern, Wallace, said, "This is Mr. Winter's visitor, Mr. Dobbs." Then he stood back a pace.

"Might I have your name?" asked the man in the blue suit.

"Franz Loebek. You are—?"

"Did Mr. Winter ask you to visit him here?"

"No, I called a number he had given me. They told me he was in this hospital."

"Then you are an old friend of Winter's?"

"We were in the same Squadron during the war. May I ask who you are, and the purpose of these questions?"

"I am a sergeant of police." Dobbs held out his hand and showed in his palm an official badge. "The purpose of the questions is to establish the reason for Winter's being here."

"Surely, that is simple enough. The man is extremely ill."

"So ill he cannot tell us what caused his sickness."

"I do not understand. He told me he had been diagnosed as a cancer case."

Wallace said sharply, "Cancer can be caused. Caused by an external agent, I mean."

"Mr. Loebek, how recently had you seen Winter before he came into this hospital?"

"Not for three months."

"What did you know of him? What was his business?"

Franz smiled. "About his business, I cannot say. He told me something of it, but I knew nothing directly. You cannot ask me to give hearsay evidence, Sergeant."

"How well did you know Winter?"

"Overseas I knew him as an officer knows a good sergeant. When I came to this country I met him once, for a drink. That is all."

"Can you tell me anything about his other friends in this city? Where and how he lived, where he usually ate, whether he had any enemies?"

"I asked him if there were any friends or relatives I could bring to visit him. He said, 'No one in this city.' I know nothing more than that."

"You cannot think of anyone who might have wished to kill him, to poison him?"

"Good God, how can you poison a man and give him cancer?"

"I leave that to the doctors," Dobbs said stolidly. "They say it's possible. And they think there's something funny about his case, which is why we were called here."

"Something funny! Something fantastic! Can Winter tell you nothing?"

"I haven't asked Winter any questions. He's too sick to be alarmed or disturbed. But the doctors have been unable to get anything from him."

"And yet they suspect something?"

"I don't know quite what they suspect." Dobbs sounded glum. "I only know I can't get much in the way of information. I've been waiting for Winter's visitors, to question them. You have been his only visitor in two days, and you can't tell me anything. Thank you for answering my questions."

"Of course," Franz said. He turned. Wallace had left the room and was walking down the long corridor. "Pardon me," Franz said. He followed Wallace.

"Dr. Wallace!"

The intern looked back. He halted.

"What is this—this foolishness?"

Wallace frowned. "Not foolishness," he said. "Something very funny. Very funny."

"Something must be damned funny, for a man with cancer to be thought the victim of poisoning."

"Not impossible, you know." Wallace led the way, walking slowly as he talked, to a small reception room with cold, shiny green leather chairs. They sat: he brought out a package of cigarettes and they began to smoke.

"To begin with, Winter is something of a hypochondriac. He has been a patient of one of our senior consultants for several years. Always running in for an examination, nothing ever seriously wrong with him.

"Less than a month ago he had a complete physical check, including X-rays. Absolutely clear. Early this week he experienced violent stomach pains, was admitted to this hospital, and operated on. The operation showed an advanced carcinoma of the stomach, which had progressed to the point where surgery was pointless."

"I have always understood that stomach cancer was of very rapid growth and that—"

"But such rapidity as this is quite unheard of. There is nothing like it in medical annals."

"Then the X-rays of last month were no good."

"They were excellent. They were rechecked, of course, after he came into hospital. They show absolutely nothing."

"The explanation?"

"You understand that this is all completely confidential? Really, I shouldn't tell you as much as—"

"I seem to be Winter's only friend. It would be better if I know."

"There was, in the opinion of the surgeons who performed the exploratory operation, some evidence that a carcinogenic substance had been ingested."

"Carcinogenic?"

"Cancer-causing. There is quite a list of such substances. Most of the vesicants, or blistering chemicals; many coal-tar derivatives, and so on."

"Not the type of thing one would usually swallow."

"Winter had a vast collection of medicines and drugs he took religiously. These substances could be administered as capsules, in some cases even as pills."

"And he obtained some? Perhaps by accident."

"Impossible. The substances have no use in internal medicine. A pharmacist would not stock them, nor would he make up a prescription for them, in a form to be taken by mouth. Some devil, some very knowing devil, prepared them and found a way of putting them into one of Winter's bottles."

"There is evidence?"

"No, none. We examined all his remaining drugs, had them analyzed. But what else could have happened?"

Franz rubbed his forehead with his fingertips, as though

to wipe his thoughts away. He had no answer to the question.

"I'm afraid I must go," Wallace said.

"Before all this, I wanted to ask you—what are his prospects?"

Wallace frowned and shook his head. The gesture said: I am sorry. There is too much death here for me to feel this deeply, but I am sorry.

"A few days." he said. "Certainly not a week."

Scene Two

Her eyes had met his only for a minute, but they had asked him to come to her.

Leaving the hospital he had walked along Pine Avenue and then, instead of turning down the steep hill to the city, had gone up the sloping paths, up the high stairs to the top of Mount Royal. There stood the Chalet; he went toward it.

Surely a building had never been less appropriately named. The Chalet was a great stone structure with a pillared façade, a huge hall with a beamed ceiling. Inside and out it recalled a railway terminus; a very misplaced terminus, built by a lunatic where no trains could ever run. In summertime a bandshell was erected on its steps and an audience sat on the broad paved apron before it for concerts; in the winter skiers filled it, buying coffee and bottled drinks at the refreshment counter and sitting at little tables under the high dark ceiling.

Franz brought his coffee into the huge hall and saw Nicole.

She was sitting alone. Coffee and ski-mitts and a jaunty cap were on the table at her elbow. Below the oval darkness of her face, white reindeer pranced across a bright red sweater of coarse, very heavy wool. Her ski-slacks were very wide at the knee, slim at the ankle, disappearing into the small boots that were a neat complexity of straps and laces and metal clips.

Her black hair was pulled above her ears and tied at the back with a small red ribbon. Without it, her perfect face was more strikingly revealed than it had been when he first saw her in the little bar. The rounded smoothness of her forehead, the width her widely-angled cheekbones gave the oval face, the nose low-bridged and straight...

Her eyes called to him and then looked quickly, reluctantly away.

Franz came slowly toward her. The bulky sweater could not hide the fullness of her breasts, the slimness of her waist. In ski-slacks, her hips flared wide above long tapered legs.

"*Bonjour, madame.*"

"*Bonjour, monsieur*—?"

"Loebek. May we talk English? It is slightly more practised than my French."

"But of course."

"May I sit here, Mrs. Porter-Smythe?"

"Please do. You know me."

"I know your name. Only, I am afraid, because I overheard it that day in the bar."

"But you remembered." She laughed gaily, and her teeth were small and a clear white. "Now you will say something very continental and flattering to explain your remembering."

"On the contrary, remembering names is part of my business."

"Then you are a stock-broker?"

"No. A head-waiter."

He had expected some change in her manner, but could detect none.

"Do you ski?" she asked. "If you are free to walk on the mountain this beautiful day, you should be skiing. The snow is perfect, a hard crust with inches of fine, dry powder."

"I did not plan to come here. I was making a hospital visit. Afterward I climbed the mountain, almost without thinking."

"A friend is ill? Or one of your family, perhaps your—?"

Franz shook his head. "I have no family. A friend is very ill. Perhaps I have seen him alive for the last time."

In sudden sympathy, she blinked her eyes quickly. But she did not look away, nor attempt to escape the sadness his face communicated. "You will be reconciled," she said quietly. "But now you are so sombre. It is a pity you came here—to drink coffee. A glass of whisky would make you easier."

"Yes. The wartime is over. One would like to forget about death for a little while. But then—one must think about life instead."

"*Mon dieu*! Today, life is as bad as death?"

He smiled. "You forget. I have not been skiing."

She encouraged his change of mood; her smile matched his. "There will be days for you to ski. And to do many other things."

"Most times, I do not know what things I wish to do."

"You speak much too vaguely."

"Then I will be explicit. You see, I am an uprooted man. I am a humbled aristocrat. And since I am no longer able to work at my profession of being a landed gentleman, I am lost."

"This is known as a country of great opportunity. In a short time you may become a landed gentleman again."

"Madame, that is the tragedy of it. I am not a man of enterprise. Therefore, I do not belong, I do not fit into this society. If North America becomes the pattern for the rest of the world—as sometimes seems horribly likely—I will not even fit into this century."

"You wished only to be left quietly alone to practise your aristocracy?"

"Exactly. In this country, no one can understand that. I must become ambitious. I am expected to plan big and bright things for my future, and work busily toward them.

Just now, I do not do what I want to do. Some things I want to do, I cannot do; that is worse."

"Ah, a new aspect. What do you know you wish to do?"

"I will be too direct for your liking," he said, gazing soberly at her.

"No, no," she protested; but her face coloured.

"Then I may tell you I would always have remembered you, from the one time I saw you in that small bar."

"How can that be true?" she asked, with an attempt at airiness.

"I do not know. But I know that I had to enquire about you, to be sure your husband was living, find out who he was. And I found you were not only married, but a bride. So that one thing I wanted to do; the thing I wanted most to do—to see you again and again—was impossible."

"Stop! Stop, I can't let you—"

"I am sorry." He stood and she felt a tingling of desire at the smooth movement of his muscled body.

"I am head-waiter at the Chatham Hotel," he said. "I should be happier if we did not meet again. And of course, you will not wish it."

Scene Three

Winter had shrivelled in the two days since Franz' previous visit. His flesh was cadaverous grey and his hands tiny and gnarled like those of a very old little woman. But he was cheerful and not in pain.

"I made out a cheque to Cameron. Four hundred. That should give him a new start."

Franz found the cheque on the bedside table and folded it into his wallet. Winter had written it with a firm hand.

"How is my funeral?"

"All ready. Waiting for the star performer," Franz said; Winter seemed to want it that way.

"I hope it was not much trouble."

"I had only to call Bill Gladwin, who was in the Squadron. He made the arrangements."

"Let us talk about you. What is new?"

"Nothing at all. In the place where I live, a fellow refugee tried to commit suicide this week. I feel so dull that I may follow his example, and try to drink myself to death. It should not take too long if I am determined to succeed."

"You Germanic people are morbid. A Jew would not commit suicide."

"There are exceptions to that."

"Under the same circumstances, I mean. Your Jew is always a romantic, with high hope. You Germans are too matter-of-fact."

With effort he turned his head to look directly at Franz. His eyes seemed naked and staring, for his eyelashes had completely lost their colour.

"I wish to leave in your care a gambling club on LaGarde Street, just north of Ontario. It is a good house, Franz. I have no one else to leave it to. Really, there is nothing to leave. A gaming house has no status in a probate court. All that would happen, were you not to go there, is that Rosaire Beaumage would take it as his own and install someone to run it."

"I—I know nothing of that business, my old friend."

"All you will have to know is easily learned. You would render me a service. I am not dying easily, Franz. It would be harder yet to know Rosaire could add that house to his possessions when I did... Will you keep it out of his hands?"

"Rosaire already controls all gambling here, they say. I could do nothing about that."

"You might. It would be up to you. He is an adversary worthy of you, Franz. A dying man does not curse lightly. But listen: I pray Jehovah will cut short the life of Rosaire."

"Who is this monster Beaumage?"

Winter's face stiffened. The weakness of impending death was gone; he spoke like a prophet chastising a wicked people. "In all my life, Franz, I have met only one completely evil man. Selfish, weak, foolish, mistaken men—many. But Beaumage loves darkness for its own sake. His God is not power; people mistakenly think that. His God is corruption. He wants—not to rule, but to overturn. His joy is to undermine anything virtuous or good."

Winter weakened. "But you think it foolish. An old gambler talking like this."

"No. Only I do not quite understand."

"I played with some minor laws of this society. Rosaire sets himself against the basic good in man. Oh, he is not great enough to be the figure I pictured him. But, Franz —he is evil!"

And if I took your gambling house, Franz thought, I would be suborning myself to this evil. I would report to Beaumage.

Aloud he said, "I cannot decide what to do today. If I took over your house I would be starting on a path I had not thought to follow."

"Let it rest in your mind. You will do what is right."

"At least, I shall think much about it."

"If you decide against the venture, do me one last favour. After I am buried inform the police of my house. Or, no. See that some influential person informs them. At least then it will be lost to Rosaire."

"I promise to do one thing or the other."

"Then I am content."

He had tired Winter. The talk, and especially the talk of Rosaire, had drawn almost the last spark from him. Franz rose quietly, hoping to slip away. Winter's voice came again, now a whisper.

"This is a strange way to die, my friend. I must tell some-one of its strangeness."

The whisper was hollow and eerie. There seemed almost to be an echo in the little room.

"I am dying with something that contains the mystery of life and creation. Somewhere within me a little group of cells, seemingly without direction, began to grow and multiply until they finally will choke out the other cells I need for living. They were a part of me, and have become anarchists. They are growing in me like some primitive parasitic plant, creating something new—but something that must die with me. That is the difference from a child growing in the womb. This new life in me is unorganized, purposeless, doomed. Without potentialities, never to see the light. You see, Franz—two kinds of creation. An evil and a good. An anarchist and a compatible. A cancer and a child."

He drew a shuddering breath. "When I wake up again not in this world, I will ask someone. It will be a good first question to ask, wherever I am going. How can this be so? How can there be an active evil, like in kind to the active good? Long ago, religion taught that, Franz. But men have forgotten it. I had forgotten, I do not see the reason why..."

His eyes did not close, but as his voice faded to nothing he seemed to lose contact with the world. After some time Franz left him, tiptoeing away down the corridor.

He went home and to bed. In his sleep, his hearing was alert for the expected ringing of the telephone.

It came before dawn. Morris Winter had died at three.

Scene Four

The short, chubby man with fedora pushed back from his brow and sloppy overcoat flapping below his knees was quite clearly a reporter. He held a small notebook open in one hand, and a pencil daggerlike in the other. His gaze swept the lobby of the Chatham quickly and cleanly. To be complete, he needed only a blatant PRESS sign in his hatband.

Franz looked at him with little interest. He was one of several who wandered in and out of the Chatham, scouting for famous guests. When he transfixed Loebek with his keen stare and beelined for the dining-room, it was too late to retreat. It was easy to see the journalist was not coming for dinner.

"Mr. Loebek."

'Yes, sir." Automatically, the smile.

"It's taken me three or four months to catch up with you. I'd still like to know how you sneaked through St. Hubert depot without a word leaking out. Now. Can I have an exclusive interview with you? I'm Wally Burns, the *Clarion*. We made a great play of the Air Force while the war was on, and we're following it up all the way. I'll have you on the front page of the second section. With pictures. How about it?"

"I'm very busy here for another hour, Mr. Burns. Could you come back then?"

"I'll wait here in the hotel. Be in the bar."

Franz was free in a half-hour. He thought of leaving by the service door; but that would just bring the reporter back the next night, probably with a photographer. He dressed in street clothes and went to the bar.

Burns was slumped in one of the deep bar armchairs with his great overcoat cascading in waves about him. He had dropped his hat on the floor beside the chair. There were two pints of beer, one empty, one half-full, on his table. "I ordered one for you, but I got thirsty," he said. "Sit down." He slapped the notebook onto the table.

"It is better if I do not drink here."

"Oh, they don't like it, eh?"

"Could we go somewhere else?"

"Sure." Burns filled his glass from the bottle and downed the rest of the beer in a long swig. He wrapped himself in the coat, which seemed to go around his plump body almost twice, and they went out onto Sherbrooke. It was a gusty, blustery night, the air very cold and clear, the light of the chattering street lamps multiplied tenfold by reflection on the wind-smoothed snow surfaces. Little plumes of snow-powder danced from the top of drifts and caroused down the broad street, jigging to right and left as the wind banked around obstacles, smashing into their faces like blasts of fine, icy white sand. The night was all midnight blue and white.

They went to a little café just off Sherbrooke Street opposite the McGill campus, a college-students' bar. A sprinkling of the tables was filled by curiously assorted undergraduates, speaking in a variety of real or assumed accents, carried away by the drama or the vehemence of their talk and gesticulating broadly. The juke-box, probably the only one in the city stocked with a collection of sentimental semi-classics, played continuously—a Strauss waltz, an air from *Carmen,* a Hungarian dance, another Strauss waltz...

Burns wanted to get right down to business.

"How long have you been there at the Chatham?"

"I took the position shortly after I arrived in Montreal."

"What are your plans?"

"None. Except to stay at the Chatham."

"Huh." Burns thought for a minute, and doodled around the edge of a page. "Well, can we put it this way: can we say you're getting experience at the Chatham before opening a restaurant of your own?"

"No. I have no intention of opening my own restaurant."

"Now look, Mr. Loebek. Something is fishy. You were a great hero in the war. Everybody in this country knows all about you—why, they'd probably even remember your name if they hear it again. So, the war is over and Canada invites you to come here and live. I just read an interview you gave then. You said you were thrilled to be coming to our land of golden opportunity and promise, and you expected to do great things here."

"I did not read that interview. The reporter had a fine imagination."

"Now here you are. You're a head-waiter."

"An honourable calling."

"Yeah, but that isn't the point. That isn't—we'll have to find an angle somewhere. Suppose—"

"Suppose I give you a better story. About a man who died yesterday at the Royal Montreal hospital. An established, middle-aged man who left his business here in Montreal and volunteered for Air Force service when the war broke out. He did nothing spectacular, nothing glorious in the service—just a good job. Then he came back and immersed himself in his work again. When he was dying he had only one wish. He wanted an Air Force funeral. Now, would that not make a story?"

"Depends on who the man was."

"His name was Morris Winter."

"Mr. Loebek, you got a story, all right. 'Patriot Gambler to Have Air Force Burial'. Yes, sir. We can even call him a gambler in print—he was fined once for running a gaming house. Tell me, is Rosaire Beaumage going to be at the funeral?"

"I don't know."

"But you've heard of Beaumage? He's just the boss of the bottom half of Montreal. If we could get a picture of him at the funeral, the story's good for two columns. Rosaire is always news."

"Because he is an enterprising man?"

"Well—I suppose you might say so. They like to read about him, anyhow. Everybody likes to think he's getting away with something. Rosaire Beaumage is an example of just how much you can get away with in a place that's supposed to have laws."

Burns paused and then went on:

"The story on Winter is fine. I got to do something on you too, though. After you sit in a Canadian fighter plane and knock down sixteen Jerries you can't just vanish."

"Not even if I want to? I suppose not. Well, I will make a bargain with you. Postpone your story on me for a week, and it will be a much better story."

"So, you been holding something out on me."

"A personal matter. In confidence, I came here with certain old family treasures. For something to do, I filled in at the Chatham until I had realized some money on them. In a week I will be in an entirely new line. It would embarrass me to have the Chatham affair publicized."

"I see."

"I have been very successful in escaping recognition. I appeal to your good fellowship. Let me remain unfound for another week."

"When you blossom forth, do I get an exclusive?"

"Of course."

"Okay," Burns said magnanimously. "I'll give you a week. You know, I thought there was something fishy about it. A head-waiter! Why, there are people in this city who would be glad to make you president of a corporation."

"Yes," said Franz. "I may take them up on it."

Scene Five

It took days of inquiry, and an old staff photograph found among Winter's effects, to locate Willy Cameron. Franz found him finally in a shoddy cafeteria, slumped in a wooden chair. A cup of cold, scummed coffee sat on the chair's one broad arm.

Cameron started as Franz approached; probably he had been there for hours and was momentarily expecting to be thrown out.

"I have been looking for you."

Cameron was completely sober. He managed a smile.

"What for? What did I do now? I don't know you."

"It does not matter. Morris Winter sent me to you."

"Well, good for Morrie. He isn't as yellow as I thought. He looks for me even after he was scared off me."

"Winter is dead," Franz said.

Cameron's cheeriness vanished. Suddenly he was badly frightened. "How'd that happen?"

"He died of cancer. It developed very suddenly."

"God! I guess you never know about those things. He looked healthier than me."

Franz drew out his wallet. "I have a cheque for you. Four hundred dollars. Morrie wanted you to get away for a new start."

"Well. Well, God, I could get sentimental. Morrie was a square guy and I played straight with him. But he didn't owe me a thing. How much? Four hundred? Well!"

"What will you do?"

"God, Mac, I'll get to the States. I'm through in this town. I been living on hand-outs for a week. I hocked my overcoat to get enough change to sleep in flop-houses down on the Main. I was tryin' to get up enough guts to hop a freight out of here. In this weather they'd have chipped me off the rods in the morning with an ice-pick. Now I can get some clothes and eat again and travel in a berth. God rest Morrie. God rest his soul. I was done, Mac. He was a big-hearted bugger. Thanks for finding me."

"You will leave Montreal?"

"Yeah. How much do you know?"

"That Rosaire Beaumage has a grudge against you."

"Rosaire has put it this way: the city isn't big enough for both of us. I'm no fool. You know Rosaire."

"No. I expect I will meet him. I am going to run Morrie Winter's house."

"Yeah?"

"I have a proposition to make. I know little about this business. I do not know the men who are working in the house. If you will come back to manage it, I will give you twenty percent of the net."

Cameron looked at him unbelievingly. Then he

47

laughed. "You told me you don't know much about the business. Say, you don't even know anything about Montreal. Did Morrie give you the business to get even with you? Did he want you killed? Look, I'll spell it out for you. First, the house wasn't Morrie's to give. Just because he owned it and equipped it and operated it doesn't mean it was his. Nothing that goes on with it goes on unless Rosaire gives the high sign. Okay, maybe he'll let you take it over—if you play it right. You want me to come back there? That wouldn't just lose you the house. It would get you killed and me killed, and if you have any family it would probably get them killed too. Didn't anybody ever tell you about playing with blasting caps?"

A scrawny waiter with a large and dirty damp rag in his hand bore down on them. "You want something to eat, Mister?" he asked Franz suggestively.

"No. We are leaving."

Cameron stood in the doorway, shivering in his suitcoat. Franz hailed a cab. Cameron didn't want to drink. He wanted to go where they could get a square meal. They told the cabby to take them to a steak house on Metcalfe Street.

While they waited for their steaks Franz said, "You do not entirely understand. When I take the house over, I do not ask Rosaire's permission. I am going to run the place independently of Rosaire. That is why I can take you back."

Cameron stared at him. He thrust out his hand. "Gimme my cheque."

"Will you not help me? I need your help."

"I'd be dead too quick to be any help to you."

"I intend to fight Rosaire. Nothing will happen to you."

"No? You'd be dead too. You'd be dead too quick to do any protecting," Cameron said. "I don't know why I'm sitting here talking to you. Lightning may hit you before the steaks come. I'm a sap to wait even for the four hundred bucks."

"My name is Franz Loebek."

"Mine is Willie Cameron. I'll send a mass card to your funeral."

"I thought my name might mean something to you."

"It'll guide my eye when I'm looking down the obit column."

"I am not afraid of Rosaire Beaumage. Not after the war."

"This isn't war. Gimme my cheque. I want to go before the roof falls in. What you just said is sacrilege. I'd sooner sit through a black mass than stay in the same room with you."

"You think I cannot fight Beaumage?"

"Look, maybe you weren't frightened in the war. You knew where the enemy was and how you could get at him. Now, suppose you'd got captured and Hitler came around inspecting prisons. And you spat on him. You're still a prisoner and you're waiting for something to happen. Tell me two things. Are you scared? And do you think you can put up a fight?"

"But, my friend, we have not been captured, and we can fight. We need only a little courage."

"I haven't got it. Anyway, you don't know what you're doing. You don't know Rosaire. You can't just draw a small circle and tell Rosaire to keep on his own side. The only way you could do something Rosaire Beaumage didn't want you to do is smash him. He doesn't let anybody set up independent and keep him out. He takes that kind of thing for a challenge to a grudge fight. He'd get you in the end, don't make any mistake about that. He doesn't forget."

"But I will crush him in the end," Franz said. "That is what I intend to do."

"Holy Mother of God. And how will you do that?"

"I can't do it alone. That is why I need you. With two, it is comparatively safe."

"Go on. I won't do it, but I want to hear how crazy you are."

"First of all: the club is closed. That is easy. We let it be known that Morrie has left a letter with an influential person; if the club is not closed down, the police will be instructed to raid it."

"All right. The place closes down. Rosaire moves all the equipment out."

"No, because he will expect to open it again after the matter has blown over. But we will anticipate him, After the passing of a little time, we move back in. Slowly the house opens again—but not to its old customers. I will bring new ones."

"Where'll you find 'em?"

"Enough that I can. The idea of this is that we will gain a little time. Rosaire will not expect anyone to reopen the house without his permission. And if I plan carefully enough, he will not know immediately that it has been reopened."

"Yeah, and you know how long a thing like that can be kept quiet. Maybe we'd get two weeks. Maybe."

"Rosaire finds, then, that someone is running the house—without his say-so. From this point, until we become strong enough to defy him, is the critical period. It is the period of the bluff."

"It's a critical period, all right. For us. Rosaire comes in for a little talk. He brings sixteen friends. After a few days, our families begin looking for us."

"He can come with six hundred friends. He won't find *us*. That is the bluff. Cameron, we could work this way: never apart, but never together. I am there, yes; but he finds only you."

"If I was going to be there—and I'm not—I wouldn't want him to find just me. Believe me, I wouldn't."

"I will always be in the club with you, Willie. But I will be there as a guest. Any trouble, I will handle. Rosaire will not know who he is fighting; that is the essential thing. We will make sure he knows someone is behind you, but he is not to know who nor how powerful that person is."

"And what happens when he takes me away for a little talk?"

"If the bluff is good enough, he won't."

"And if the bluff isn't good enough?"

"It will be."

"You got to prove it to me."

"I do not say we will frighten Rosaire. But we will make him wish to exercise caution. We will make it seem to him that the house is being run by a very important personage. Before he acts, he will need to know more about that. We will see that he learns nothing. There is something to be said for the very audacity of this scheme. Rosaire knows his own reputation. He will be sure that no amateur would try a hand against him. He will be sure that you would not defy him without extraordinary backing. He will hesitate and be lost. What do you say to it?"

"Gimme my cheque."

"Morrie Winter treated you well. This is what he wanted, and I cannot do it without you."

"I don't want to go see Morrie. I want to see more of life."

Franz had argued enough. "Oh, all right."

"You know, I wonder something," Cameron mused. "I wonder if Rosaire fixed it so Morrie would get cancer?"

"Why do you say that?" Franz shot back to him.

"Why I—was just kidding."

"Did Rosaire know Morrie hated him?"

"I didn't know that myself. But Rosaire knows everything."

"It is possible, what you said. That Rosaire killed Morrie."

"Aw, for God's sake," Cameron snickered. "Come off it!"

Scene Six

In the early morning Franz hailed a cab on Sherbrooke Street and gave the driver the address of the Frontenac Apartments.

The cabby was a lanky cowboy, handling his big car as a range rider guides his pony; folded over the wheel, he did not drive the car so much as ride it. His lean body swayed from side to side like that of a skater dodging obstacles, as he zig-zagged his machine through the heavy morning traffic, now arcing around a chugging bus, now cutting in front of another scampering taxi. Approaching Côte des Neiges corner he performed a broken-field manoeuvre that brought him into the inside lane, and coasted around the corner on a yellow light. Delicately balancing the weight of his foot against the tension of the accelerator spring, feeding fuel to his powerful engine as fast as it would rev up, gaining speed smoothly he hurtled up Côte des Neiges away from the centre of Montreal. As he curved off Cote des Neiges and more steeply upward on MacGregor, the road became icy. He shifted down to second gear with easy precision and the car sped on without a second's hesitation, climbing powerfully, curving back onto Côte des Neiges and up, past Cedar. He slowed as he approached Westmount Boulevard and swung the car to the right, up a driveway that led to a high apartment building towering over the Côte road at the very side of Mount Royal. He stopped smoothly, unfolded himself from behind the wheel, and opened the door for Franz.

Franz paid the meter reading and tipped him a dollar.

"*Votre nom?*"

"Jules. Jules Trebonne, m'sieur."

"You are a radio cab. If I called your company, would I always be able to get you?"

The cabby looked at his dollar. He was a thin, long-faced Frenchman incapable of smiling, but he was glumly happy.

"From anywhere in the city, m'sieur. Ask for me by my number. *Six-cent-treize.*"

"*Oui. Salut.*"

"*Salut, m'sieur.*"

The supervisor was not a janitor, nor the overseer of

janitors. He was a combination rental agent and hotel manager. He was a correct little man with a starchily-pressed sack suit and a very stiff white collar. He had watery blue eyes and very thin hair brushed carefully back to cover his considerable baldness; his accent was not quite Cockney.

"What was your name again, sir?"

"Loebek. Franz Loebek."

"I'll be glad to put you on our list, Mr. Loebek. But I'm afraid I can't hold out any great hope. Perhaps a year from this spring—"

"Mr. Gladwin was kind enough to recommend these apartments to me. I am sorry you have no vacancy."

"Was that—Mr. Justice Gladwin, sir?"

"Mr. William Gladwin."

"I see. I should hate to disoblige a friend of young Mr. Gladwin's. I tell you, sir, there *is* one apartment on the third floor. We have been reserving it for a gentleman from Argentina, but there seems to have been some difficulty about his visa. I have about given him up, and of course one can't wait forever. Now if you would care to inspect the apartment—"

"This third floor suite is your only vacancy?"

"Oh, yes," the little man said with something like triumph. "Except of course the penthouse. The penthouse has been vacant for some months."

"Which is larger?"

"All the apartments are the same size, sir." He recited: "Drawing-room, dining salon, master bedroom with bath, second bedroom with bath, library, butler's pantry, kitchen, servant's quarters. Of course, the penthouse is—er, dearer," he concluded.

"I will inspect the penthouse."

They went up sixteen floors in a self-service elevator. The superintendent inserted his key in a severe grey door and bowed Franz in. The door led through a short entry to a long, low drawing-room exquisitely furnished and decorated in grey and scarlet. At the far end of the room, floor-length windows and French doors gave on a terrace and, beyond, the city which lay far below them. The decor was sumptuous, modern but not extreme.

"The suite was decorated for its last tenant, the Comte de Maligne. When you wish, of course, your own furniture can be—"

"I have just come from abroad. My effects are not in Canada."

"Then, should you decide to lease, we will decorate in whatever style you prefer."

"I do not care to set my taste against that of the Comte. This room is entirely satisfactory. Is any renovating required?"

"Only thorough cleaning."

"Have it done this afternoon. I wish to be here tomorrow evening."

When he came out into the sun and snow again Jules Trebonne, *six-cent-treize*, was still waiting with his cab at the door. He emerged from the cab and played footman to Franz.

The car was a navy blue Buick with rolling, powerful lines. Jules nursed its power carefully and started away smoothly.

"I waited," he volunteered diffidently. "It is a quiet day. Too sunny. Too many walking."

"Ah," said Franz, stretching comfortably in the seat, "who would not prefer to ride?"

"Ride, yes. Drive, no. It is not good for the nerves."

"That is because other drivers have not your skill."

Jules was unable to grin, but he touched his cap in acknowledgement.

Franz asked suddenly, "Do you know of Rosaire Beaumage?"

The driver shrugged. "Who is he?"

"An important man in Montreal."

"Oh," Jules said, "I am not of Montreal. I came here from Quebec a few months ago."

Scene Seven

Each person who had described Rosaire Beaumage to Franz had elaborated on the manner of man he was, without speaking of his appearance or personal characteristics. Each of these persons had known or seen Rosaire over a period of years and had come to take for granted that such a character reposed in such a body. Franz had pictured Beaumage as heavy and dark, middle-aged and prosperously rotund, greasy with evil. No one had thought to set right this mental image.

In the little memorial chapel where Morris Winter's body had been carried for last rites, Franz took his place in a pew beside Willie Cameron. "There's Rosaire," Cameron said.

Beaumage was a quietly dressed, very ordinary youngish man. It was not possible, as it usually is, to tell at a glance whether he was English or French-Canadian. He bore the mark of neither the demagogue nor the brute on his face. Where a man with more regard for his appearance would have cultivated a moustache to draw attention from his slightly protuberant front teeth, Rosaire was clean-shaven. The effort to keep his lips neatly closed over these teeth gave his mouth a slightly set, strained look. His dark brown hair was thin and limp; it was untidy, but not overlong. His nose was sweeping and powerful, with a broad square tip.

His eyes alone were impressive. They were small, of a very bright fluorescent blue, and they missed nothing. He gave the impression of a misplaced seminarian, a man who, had he chosen the Church, would have been a priest of shallow but intransigent faith.

The coffin was carried from the deathlike darkness of the funeral chapel into the bright sun and clean snow, the blue sky and clear air of Montreal in February. Six men in Air Force sergeants' uniforms lifted Winter's body to the back of an open truck. The flag was over his coffin.

The band was drawn up in open formation, the files spread from one curb to the other. The sombre note of a muted cymbal smote and shivered on the cold still air and was choked, and smote again. The truck began to creep forward and the men marched stiffly, deliberately, one step, then a pause, then at the dead beat of the muffled drum a step again. The brasses spoke with firm, mourning minor chords. They played the Dead March from *Saul*, deliberately, matching the slow march of the men who walked with downcast eyes.

Winter had been right. This was sadness, but a sorrow without wailing. It was solemnity dignified, not besotted by gloom. It was a direct appeal to emotion, a scene that touched upon the sympathetic nerves like the full-dress playing of a loved national anthem. But it did not depress; it uplifted, it thrilled, and if there were tears they came from a feeling more like inspiration than like grief.

At this moment, Rosaire Beaumage laughed. It was a loud laugh, so that heads turned in his direction, but it was not a nervous laugh of strain. It was a guffaw of pure enjoyment.

Franz was nearby. He could hear Rosaire speak to the man beside him in soft French: "It is to be hoped Morrie knows what is going on. This he would love. *Regard!* The parade will hold up the traffic on St. Catherine Street for ten minutes." Rosaire looked down the street, chuckling.

The brief procession passed on to the next block. The knot of people by the curb began to break up. Willie Cameron came to speak to Franz. "Who laughed?"

"Beaumage."

"Bastard."

Cameron swallowed nervously. Rosaire was walking away, and he followed the man with his eyes. He was ready to turn his head quickly if Rosaire glanced toward them.

"I've been thinking over your idea," he told Franz.

"It does not matter. I am making other plans."

"Don't brush me off now. Maybe I've changed my mind."

"I do not want you."

"You wanted me last night."

"Now I do not want you. You are too afraid."

"Listen, you said twenty percent of the net, didn't you? I'm getting less scared all the time."

"Will you do exactly as I say?"

"You're the boss all the way through. I think maybe you can do it. If I didn't I wouldn't take the chance."

"You know who is running Winter's house now?"

"A frog called Maurice."

"I will have someone get in touch with him. I will make sure the house is closed. It will stay closed for a week. You are to stay under cover for that time. Then, call Information and get my number. I will have more instructions for you."

Cameron walked quickly away, and Franz turned. He had stepped out to cross the street when a car accelerating rapidly cut in front of him, forcing him back to the curb. The car was a black Lincoln limousine, driven by a uniformed chauffeur. In the tonneau were Rosaire and two other men.

Rosaire was still chuckling.

Scene Eight

"You told me to call you when I had changed my mind," Franz said.

Bill Gladwin was surprised. "I didn't really expect you to call, you were acting so damned independent. What would you like to do?"

"I have already acted. I have leased the penthouse of the Frontenac; I am moving there this evening."

"The penthouse? You *have* done it. That's fine. Wonderful." He paused. "Tell you what," he resumed suddenly, "I've just the right occasion to introduce you. Dinner party I'm giving the end of this week; Friday. At Father's place, he indulges me in these little fancies. You come, and afterward you can suggest we adjourn to your flat. I'll back you up. You can show it off."

"Thank you very much. That would be fine."

"Anyone else recognize you at the Chatham?"

"No one except a journalist. I postponed him."

"Then the Chatham is a closed incident."

"Miss Warren came back once and spoke to me. She tried to be offensive."

"Ah, good old Linda. Don't worry. I'll take care of her."

"Could you do me a further favour?"

"Of course, name it."

"This is in the line of your business. It may be slightly illegal, but it is not a thing that would cause you trouble. You know Rosaire Beaumage?"

"I know who he is. Do you?"

"I do. I wonder if you would phone Rosaire for me? You need not identify yourself, except as the lawyer of the late Morris Winter. Please say to Rosaire that unless the gambling house formerly run by Winter is closed, the police will be given all the details about it and asked by several influential citizens to close it."

"That," Gladwin said, amused, "is a rum errand."

"Winter was in the Squadron. You are not likely to remember him—a sergeant. I was with him shortly before he died, and his wish was that the house should not fall to Rosaire."

"Winter—of course. You asked me about arranging his funeral. All right, I'll be glad to do it. I phone Rosaire, and"—he went through the message again to make sure he had it correct.

"Thanks. That is right. I shall look forward to Friday evening."

"At seven-thirty," Gladwin said. "Cheers."

Franz left the telephone booth and took his place at the dining-room door. Carl handed him the reservations list and moved to his own position, at the side of the serving table near the door.

"So, it is the last night," Carl said. "Where are you going? You have not told us."

"I have no new place yet. I think I shall look around for a different kind of work. I am tired of butling."

"Who is taking your place?"

"I don't know. The manager was enraged. He wanted me to give two weeks' notice."

Carl's moonlike face wrinkled in a smile. "I may be head-waiter for a few days. But I am too much of a peasant to suit them. Later they will get some other exiled Count with a properly haughty manner."

"Have I been that bad?"

"Ah, no. That good. It is a gift, like the gift for the theatre. The show must be put on for the guests, who pay to see it—the gracious smile, the easy bow; the grand flourish of opening the menu. The imperious snapping of fingers to bring the servile waiter scurrying to the table. A good waiter, of course, expects and appreciates this display... But, hold on. Guard your temper on this last night—here comes your friend."

Linda Warren was crossing the lobby toward them, dressed superbly in a strapless evening gown of watered magenta silk. The bodice was low-cut and very tight, the skirt full. Her long blonde hair fell to her bare shoulders. She was alone.

Franz took a long breath. He bowed stiffly and said, "Good evening, Miss Warren." He did not smile.

"I'm not coming for dinner. I just dropped by to say I was sorry."

"Sorry for what, Miss Warren?"

"That reporter. Burns, I think his name was. He was interviewing me about some Junior League work and some-how your name came out. It was stupid of me to tell him you were here, but really—the man was asking ten questions a second. I'm afraid I got confused and told him."

"Oh? It is hard to imagine you confused, Miss Warren. But in any case—I have seen no reporters. So you see, there is no need to apologize."

"I—see," she said slowly. "Well, no harm done. I was afraid I'd committed an awful crime; Bill Gladwin made it seem as though your being here was a state secret. Almost as if you were doing espionage."

"He merely wished to spare me unpleasant publicity."

"Of course. Although the publicity would have been most pleasing to the hotel, I imagine. Surely it would have increased your value to them?"

"That is a consideration, I grant, despite my personal feelings. But it does not matter now. You see, I was here only until some of my affairs were settled. This is my last night at the hotel."

"Oh, what a shame! Such a wonderful head-waiter. Don't you like the work?"

"I will miss it very much. But I must try to improve my position. When I am established in other circumstances, perhaps Mr. Gladwin will bring you to see my home."

"Oh, don't wait for Gladwin," she said carelessly. "Ask me yourself."

Franz bowed.

"Don't worry about Charles, by the way. He won't re-member you were here. He was sozzled, as usual."

"Charles? I'm afraid you confuse me again."

"Charles Porter-Smythe. With me the other night. I thought I'd introduced him."

"No. You merely introduced me."

The ironic quality of his tone gave her no further open-ing for comment. She turned and walked toward the bar, thinking: God damn Burns! He promised he'd get the story. She was enraged, of course, not half so much by Burns' failure as by being made a fool in front of Franz.

And Franz thought: Charles Porter-Smythe! So that is how he spends an evening. If he is making a practice of neglecting Nicole, then…

THREE

Scene One

THE FEBRUARY SUN, LAZY about getting up, was yet not as lazy as Franz. Light from the dull, misted sky slanted onto the tiled deck of the terrace and was reflected into the room, falling on the wide bed where he sprawled asleep.

The seascapes spaced about the walls were the keynote of the bedroom's blue-and-sand decorative scheme. They were hard, realistic oils of a lashed and bitter ocean jarring on a ragged basalt coast. Le Comte de Maligne had loved the sea. Franz had made no change in the room save to indulge an idiosyncrasy and move the bed to the exact centre of the floor.

Flung on the aquamarine rug beside the bed was a dress shirt, topped by a twisted white tie. About the back of a straight chair was an evening jacket, and trousers lay neatly folded across the seat. A heavy table, running the width of the bed, stood at its head. On it Franz had scattered a pack of Players' cigarettes and a silver lighter; change, bills, and a pigskin wallet. There was also a cut-glass ashtray, a small radio, and a telephone. A pad beside the telephone was scribbled over with numbers, and the notation: "Elite Catering. Marius."

The telephone rang.

Franz had been lying on his stomach, head deep in the pillow, his eyes open and clear. It rang again, and he lifted the phone from the cradle.

"Hello."

"Franz! Bill. Say, good show. Haven't so much enjoyed an evening in years. You're in, definitely in, as far as that crowd's concerned. Annette was raving about you all the way home—what did you say to her?"

"Annette? I don't quite—"

"My little French blonde with the round face. You'll remember the names after you've met them a few more times. Well, Annette went on for a long time. You have the manners of a White Russian prince, the appearance of a character from a better Noel Coward play, the physique of a Christian slave who has conquered several lions, the—"

"Hold, hold."

"Well—Annette is a bit enthusiastic. But frankly, I thought you did a wonderful job. Everyone was in a stodgy mood after we left my place—the cook should know better than to serve a dessert as heavy as that pudding. Those drinks were a real inspiration—light, and heady. What was in them?"

"Cointreau, I think. I don't really know. The man did them."

"Then he's a real find. Be sure you keep him."

"He was engaged only for the evening," Franz said, and a scowl unreflected in his voice crossed his face.

"Too bad. However, you didn't really need him. You made the party move from the moment we came into your apartment. Now, what next?"

"What do you suggest?"

"I doubt if I need to suggest anything. I expect you'll get several invitations from last night's crowd before the day's over. However, meanwhile, I'll do two things. If I'm invited to anything interesting I'll see that you're asked to come with me. And I'll scout job openings for you."

"You need not press that too strongly. I am content to sit back and wait for a while."

"I'll just sniff the wind for you. Now, is there anything else? Anything I can do?"

"Come around and have a drink whenever you feel like it. I hardly had a chance to talk with you last night."

"Gladly. Probably tomorrow, before dinner. And what else? Oh, I know. Money. After all, this thing was my idea and I'd expect you'll be in pretty deep before the pelf starts rolling in. Let me help in that."

"Well—I am not anxious to mention that problem. But—"

"Of course! Don't hesitate."

Franz took a deep breath. "I have a venture that seems most attractive. I am thinking of making it, and that is why I am not too anxious to take a job from one of your friends. But it would require—"

"How much? I can scare it up on short notice."

"Ten thousand dollars."

"Ten—well, that would take a little time. I—ah, I guess I'd have to know a little about the venture."

"Of course," Franz said. "Though the money would be returned in almost no time. It is in the nature of a stake."

"If the business is good enough to pay it back right away, I wouldn't want the money taken out. I'd like to keep an interest."

"You can buy yourself a ten percent interest in my venture for your ten thousand. What do you say?"

"Tell me about it."

"It is a business-like undertaking, bound to succeed because there is a constant demand for the service offered."

"More detail. After all, the last time we talked you were telling me you were a babe in the woods, as far as North American business is concerned. How do I know—perhaps you'll be buying gold bricks, or the Jacques Cartier bridge?"

"Ah, you wrong me. I can tell you this: the business is more in the nature of selling gold bricks."

"Is it legal?"

"It is tolerated."

For a few moments there was no sound from the other end of the line. Then Gladwin said, "All right, dammit, ten thousand. I'll take the chance. And I want ten percent of the venture. Tell me what bank you want it deposited in."

After these arrangements were completed, Franz hung up the phone. He sat up, explored the floor for his slippers, and finding them made his way from the bedroom, down a corridor, into the great grey and scarlet drawing-room. Had a grenade been exploded in the center of the room, it could not have been more littered. Franz shook his head and moved on.

From the drawing-room a short passageway led toward the kitchen. On one side, an open door revealed the butler's pantry. Opposite was another door, which Franz opened to reveal a small bedroom.

A heavy man completely dressed in dinner clothes slumbered on the narrow bed. He was flat on his back, his arms folded on his chest. His shoes were scuffed, and in the sole of one was worn a great, round hole.

Franz lifted a leg and kicked the man's foot twice. "Stir yourself!" he commanded. "You have not moved since I carried you here last night. Come, drunken pig!"

The man was almost completely bald. He had a soft, rounded face on which a growth of black whisker had appeared during the night. His nose was hooked in the regal, sweeping fashion of an old Assyrian king, and his eyelashes were very long. They rested on his cheeks, with no quiver to indicate they might rise to unveil his eyes.

"Marius!" Franz shouted. He grasped the footboard and shook the bed.

The man awoke then, and gazed at him calmly. "Herr von Loebek," he said absently. "Or—was it Count von Loebek? I fear my memory is poor."

"Get up!"

"I humbly beg your pardon, Excellency. Were I able, I should cringe to the floor and lick your boots. But—"

"Less talk, man. Up, and set to work on the apartment. It's a shambles."

Marius laughed.

"You fool, do you really wish to lose your job?"

"I assure you, I've lost it already. I was on final trial

with my friend the caterer, and could not return to him without a glowing letter of recommendation which you will never give... But I laugh at you. You have no experience in handling North American servants, that is completely clear. First, you must bring me a cup of hot tea. Then we will discuss what I am to do."

"How much of this insolence do you think I will endure? Up, off this bed before I—"

Marius stretched lazily. "I am getting up. But this is not insolence, merely a desire to help you. My own servants were treated far more strictly than you would treat me. And benefited from it. There are no good servants in this country."

"Am I meant to guess?" Franz asked with irony. "Marius—Baron of Poland, perhaps?"

"Ah, no." Marius slowly rocked his body to an upright position at the side of the bed. "Merely a second cousin to the little white father, the Czar of all the Russias ... I see I am completely dressed. That is convenient."

"You have not the face of a Russian. You are a Jew."

"I have an international face," Marius said pleasantly. "It is well, because I have wandered internationally. Sometimes I believe I have been wherever my race has been... I am a Jew, of course, or partly a Jew. That does not alter the fact that I am a Prince of Russia. Where is the bathroom?"

Franz laughed. "You will find it beyond the drawing-room, my prince," he said, gesturing politely. His normal good humour had returned. "When you have washed, return to the kitchen and in the absence of servants we will make ourselves a breakfast."

When Marius returned coffee was percolating on the stove, large tumblers of grapefruit juice stood on the kitchen table, and Franz was drawing golden toast from the toaster.

"You do better than I," Marius said graciously. "I invariably burn the toast."

"Of what use are you, then, as a servant?"

"Little. But then, I am of little use at all."

"Our minds run the same paths. I also have felt useless in this country."

"Ah, but I am useless anywhere. Are you a sot?"

Loebek smiled. "No. At least, not yet."

"You saw how I behaved last night."

"You behaved excellently throughout the evening. I could not have done without you. Only after the guests had gone—complete collapse."

"It is usual."

"You know your fault. You can cure it."

"Impossible. I must live with it, like a man who has married poorly must live with his shrew. But no matter. Let us eat, and then I will sweep up the debris and go."

"Go where?"

"I have no idea. Perhaps you would care to tip me for my services last night. In that case I would postpone all problems for another day."

"You need not go at all. I must have someone here to care for this apartment."

"I have warned you about my habits."

"I will take a chance on them."

"They are not really as bad as I have said. To work for you would be a stroke of good luck. I may be sober for days."

"You will be sober until I pay you. That will not be for some time."

"Good," said Marius cheerfully. "And put your liquor behind a stout lock."

Scene Two

C. C. Warren stared at the world through a pair of horrid magnifying spectacle lenses that made his eyes twice life-size and gave him the appearance of an inquisitive beetle.

He was a short man with a neat, rounded corporation and spindle legs who habitually moved at a dignified trot.

He trotted now into his oak-panelled dining-room, helped himself to a steaming kipper from a covered dish on the buffet, and sat down at the head of a table long enough to seat a score. After a minute, Linda came into the room.

Warren looked up from his *Gazette* and admired her. His daughter was dressed in riding breeks and long, glistening boots. She wore a dark green shirt of soft wool, a shirt that was almost too tight for her firm breasts and wide shoulders.

"Morning, Linda."

"Hi, Father."

"Where are you riding?"

"On Mount Royal. Annette said I could take her mount. She's too lazy to exercise him, really."

"I envy you."

"Come along. We'll find you a horse."

"Too busy. Always too busy, my dear."

"What are you doing today that can't wait?"

"Setting up a new company, I think," Warren said absently, his bug-eyes back on the financial page.

"Large company?"

"No, just a baby. My chemical outfit got a license to make an English plastic material, and I think it will do better on its own. So we'll set up a subsidiary."

"Hmm. Want a good man for it?"

"Certainly." Warren looked up. "I'm always wanting a good man. Who?"

"Oh"—she waved airily. "Friend of a friend."

"When did you start getting jobs for friends of friends?"

"Frankly, this is someone who intrigued me."

"What's his name?"

"I don't quite remember. I'd never heard the name before. He's a Count or Baron from somewhere in Europe."

"I have a number of those," Warren said teasingly, "working as clerks and book-keepers."

"This one was also a Squadron-Leader in the R.C.A.F. He was quite a hero during the war, according to Bill Gladwin."

"That promotes him, in my mind. I can offer him a junior salesman's job."

"How long is it since I asked for a favour?" she said angrily.

"The end of last month, when your account was over-drawn."

"A favour like this."

"I must admit, a few of your ex-admirers are on my payroll."

"Then you might at least see this man."

"All right, I shall. Send him to me."

"He seems to have a remarkable amount of pride. I think I'd better keep out of it entirely. Will you phone Bill Gladwin? Bill can send him to you."

"Certainly. Does it satisfy you if I make him manager of a corporation—a rather small corporation?

"Oh, yes." She tossed her head. "But I doubt if it would satisfy him."

"Just what do you mean by that? Does he already have a responsible position?"

"The last time I saw him he was a head-waiter."

"Well—really!"

"But a very proud head-waiter. Don't forget that. And please, Father, I don't want this loused up."

"Do you want to go back to school, young lady? Try to use civilized language."

She bowed her head meekly. "Will you endeavour to see that no impediment delays the execution of this assignment?"

Warren laughed. "All right, my dear. But," he became very serious, "I don't want an ex-count, ex-waiter, graduate gigolo in my family. Remember that. You worry me a little.

You're not usually so intense, my dear."

Linda shrugged. "Oh, well, if you're going to be silly about this thing—forget it. I doubt if he needs a job from you, anyway."

"I'll see him," Warren grumbled. "I rather want to see him, now. I'll call Bill Gladwin."

"I know!" Linda said suddenly. "Ask Bill to bring him to our cocktail party Saturday. I've invited Bill."

"Then it's your department to tell Bill to bring him."

"I'm the social department. This is business."

"Oh, no. I don't do business at my parties. I'll just meet him and perhaps talk to him."

"You'd better do more than that. I doubt if he'd come around to your office, unless you'd made him some kind of offer."

"Ridiculous. He'll know who I am."

"But he won't be impressed. Oh, I want to see this!"

Scene Three

It had been snowing all afternoon, laying a gauzy carpet of white over the roofs and yards of Westmount. Nicole had pulled high, fleece-lined boots over her useless little party shoes, wrapped herself in an old fur coat and was kicking her way happily up the long slope to the Warren mansion.

Kick, kick... The snow fluttered up from the toes of her boots and settled slowly again, almost as light as when it had first fallen... I'm late, she thought, late (kick), late (kick), late. And I don't care. Perhaps I won't go. I'll walk right on past the Warrens' and go to Westmount lookout, and see the snow on this city. Then I'll climb through the snow in the park to the very top of the mountain. I want to be alone...

Alone, and think of what? The ruin of my life? The idiocy of being married to Charles...? She was beginning to feel certain now that she would never have a child by Charles. That seemed really like the final judgement on their marriage.

She stopped before the carefully shovelled and swept front walk of the Warrens' great house. Dusk was falling, blue on the white new snow, and the lights of the house shone yellow. Shadows moved against the windows. She shrugged and turned to go in.

Nicole opened the great front door and entered without ringing the bell. The high entrance rotunda was pillared in white marble, with a black marble floor and a ceiling almost obscured by a huge, graceful crystal chandelier.

She stamped the snow from her great boots, then with a tiny grimace of guilt kicked it to the wall. Walking down the corridor toward the stairs she came upon C. C. Warren, sitting at the telephone table below the stairway. It was dim here and her impression was of two circles of glass, each filled with the huge distorted image of an eye. The Cheshire cat and his grin, Nicole thought; the St. James Street coyote and his eyes...

"No," Warren said into the telephone. "Absolutely impossible... Of course, you may tell him I'm sorry, but don't apologize. I don't care if he came from Samarkand by rocket, I can't see him until Monday. His office will just have to get along without him....Well, *get* him a hotel reservation, then; phone Marvin at the Ritz... Come, you can handle this yourself. No? Well, get him to the phone, then. I'll wait."

The blue bug-eyes fastened themselves on Nicole. "My dear! Excuse me. Idiots that show up for a noon appointment at five-thirty."

"At least you keep business out of your leisure hours," Nicole said teasingly. "I thought all you great tycoons worked day and night, throughout the week."

Warren winked. The effect was like the drawing of a seamy curtain over the bottom of a tumbler. "I do, my dear. It's just that this man is too important to see right away. He must be kept waiting until he... Yes?" into the telephone. "Ah, Mr. Caron. I'm sorry the storm delayed you..."

Nicole went quietly past him up the stairs and his voice faded out. She kicked off her boots, threw her coat on a bed and glanced in a mirror. She liked the way the wind had tossed her hair, and did not rearrange it.

When she came downstairs again into the long drawing-room where the cocktail guests were gathered, the first person she saw was Franz.

The cocktail party, like a cut-crystal goblet rolling along a beam of sunlight, threw out little flashes of colour, sudden motion, little sparks of laughter. Perhaps thirty people were caught in the room, pulled together as though lassoed by one large encircling rope. Be merry or morose, drink as much as you will or as little as you can manage, smoke until the ashtrays are filled and you must cast your ashes on the floor, sit or stand—but talk, talk, talk. Talk to people you love and people you hate, to friends and strangers, to people you awe and people you amuse and people you bore. But talk.

Linda was all black and white, her hair sweeping down to meet the low neck of her black moiré cocktail dress. She was talking indolently to three men, of whom Bill Gladwin was one. The round-faced Annette, at the edge of this group, looked slowly around the room for the waiter with his polished silver tray of long-stemmed glasses. Moving through the room, a bulgy little gnome in business dress, Warren nodded left, left, right, right, saying a word to each. Charles Porter-Smythe, like a drunken soldier on parade, stood with his feet precisely together and swayed irregularly—forward, catch; backward, catch; and drained a full glass and looked about him, far more anxiously than Annette, for another cocktail. His head nodded solemnly as he listened to something Franz was telling him.

Oh, God! And how to escape? Nicole asked herself.

Linda's voice rose above the undulation of noise and called to her, and she made her way carefully through the course of jutting elbows and tippable glasses and sudden unpredicted turnings to Linda and Bill.

"Darling," said Linda, "that's a most unfashionable dress you're wearing." She said this in a loud voice.

"But so becoming," interjected Gladwin.

"But—red!" Linda mouthed. "It's wintertime, in Montreal, and everyone is in mourning. One can wear only black."

Nicole smiled. Her black eyes seemed to catch and reflect much of the light in the room. She was not embarrassed, but simply amused by Linda.

"I refuse to mourn for winter. It is the only good season in Montreal. Really, one should wear white to match the snow."

With the usual fluidity of small groups in a cocktail party vortex, their circle changed. One of the extra men took Annette to meet a friend, the second drifted off to replenish his glass, and Gladwin, Linda and Nicole were left together. Linda nudged Bill and inclined her head meaningfully toward Franz.

"How did you get him to come?"

"I didn't mention who was giving the party."

"Has he met Father yet?"

"Not through me."

"I'll introduce them, as soon as he gets away from Charles. I'd better go attach myself to Father and hold him in readiness." She swirled away. Bill Gladwin signalled a waiter and presented Nicole with a cocktail.

"We were discussing Franz Loebek," he said. "There, he's talking to Charles."

Nicole nodded. She looked not at Franz but at Charles, who seemed very drunk yet was still drinking too rapidly.

"Should we join them? You and Franz have met, haven't you?"

"How did you know that?" Nicole asked sharply.

"Why, he mentioned it. Asked me whether I knew you. What's wrong?"

"Nothing. I—I wish—"

"Yes?"

Nicole's gaze went from Charles to Franz. Then she looked away, her face cleared, and she smiled at Gladwin. "Very confidentially, Bill, I wish I were not here. I wish I were just finishing a long day of skiing at Ste. Agathe."

"You also wish Charles wasn't here," he said, undeceived. "How's his problem? Getting worse?"

"Oh, please, Bill."

"Seriously, Niccy. You can purge me from your list if I'm interfering, but I know a good psychiatrist. Would you talk to him, and get Charles to see him?"

"Perhaps it has not come to that."

"Perhaps it has."

"I cannot help him because I cannot help myself," she said in a rush. "We are helpless against each other, we—"

A waiter paused before them, and they automatically took fresh glasses. "To Lethe," Bill said. They raised the drinks.

The waiter went slowly and carefully on through the throng. A conscientious and observant man, he picked a path that would take him in a broad arc beyond Charles Porter-Smythe's reach. But Charles' eyes met his before he could evade the glance, and he was summoned with an imperious finger. Charles took a new cocktail; Franz refused.

Charles wore a wide, fatuous grin, half of drunkenness, half of genuine amusement. "Go on, please go on," he told Franz.

Franz smiled at his own recollections. "Of course, no one could find a screwdriver in the entire village. But the senior pilot was by this time entirely determined. Nothing would do but that he must play the harp. So finally, they took the grand piano apart with a claw-hammer. Very few of the strings were broken. They stood the frame upright

73

on the floor and he gave his concert from midnight till dawn. His playing was angelic."

"Lord, I wish I'd had evenings like that! What a bunch you must have had." He was suddenly morose. "They turned me down, you know. Wouldn't even accept me for home duty. I couldn't even find out the reason. Some medical idiocy."

"It is all just memory now."

"Ah, yes, yes," Charles nodded gravely. His head rolled a little. "But look, you must tell me some more. About how you came here, what you intend doing—let's get out of this."

"It would be rude to leave the party, I'm afraid. If—"

"Oh, I don't mean leave here. Bar downstairs. Rumpus room. But very quiet just now. Rumpus is all up here, heh? C'mon."

Charles led the way to the door, down the corridor to a heavily-carpeted flight of stairs that led into a dim basement play-room. The walls were tastefully muralled with scenes of Montreal as they might be viewed from a Sherbrooke Street sidewalk café, and there were deep red-leather chesterfields and chairs. Franz sat in a chair, and Charles plumped his narrow body awkwardly onto a chesterfield.

"There's a plot against me," Charles said bitterly.

"A plot?"

"I own a little business, you see. Nuts and screws. M' father's firm. But s'full of all the people who worked for my father. Now they all seem to think they're working for 'emselves. Pay no attention to me. 'S a plot."

"A difficult thing to combat," Franz agreed.

"I never knew enough about the business. Now they won't tell me. 'S a—a conspiracy of silence, that's what it is. Know what I need? Need a liaison man. Someone who will be firm. I'm too kind to the bastards. Need an—an assistant general manager, that's what I need. Now, you're not settled in any place here yet, are you?"

"I regret my time is not entirely free," Franz told him. "I am not associated with a firm, but I have a number of personal transactions to carry out. They are keeping me quite occupied. I am afraid it would do no good to discuss this at the present time."

Franz paused. As he had been speaking Charles had drained his cocktail glass, leaned far over to the end of the chesterfield to place it on a small table, and—sunk to a prone position. His eyes were closed. His breathing was quiet and peaceful.

"Good old Charles," said a cynical female voice.

Franz looked up. Linda Warren came into the bar, accompanied by a middle-aged man whose eyes were great staring horrors behind magnifying lenses.

"I wonder if Charles will spend the night here?" Linda asked idly. "Probably, unless we apply physical violence. Mr. Loebek, I was looking for you. I wanted to introduce my father."

Franz stood. The man with the magnified eyes stared for a minute, disgustedly, at Charles Porter-Smythe. He turned then to Franz. His expressionless eyes could show no sentiment, but the lines of his face relaxed into a pompously cordial expression. "Mr. Loebek! William Gladwin has been telling me about you. I may say I am honoured, really honoured to have you as a guest in my home."

Franz shook his hand. Linda saved the necessity of a reply by asking, "What shall we do with the body?"

"He should recover in a few minutes," Franz told her. "In any case, I will aid him. One's Air Force experience is useful in such cases."

"Good. I'll get back to the howling mob." She shot a hard glance at her father, and left the bar.

"Will you allow me?" Warren led Franz toward the broad mahogany bar at the back of the room. "There is some really fine Scotch here. I wish we'd come down before you tasted those little horrors one is expected to serve

75

upstairs." He went behind the bar and began clumsily mixing two highballs. "I am sorry to say," he went on, "that Linda and I unintentionally eavesdropped at the door for a minute. It seemed that Charles was offering you a job."

Franz smiled. "It was a little hard to tell, but that seemed his intention. I was erecting the appropriate defenses so that I could refuse the offer."

"Then you are not interested in employment?"

"Unfortunately, my own affairs are pressing."

"I'd hoped you would call at my office next week and have a chat with me. Perhaps you will, in any case. I promise I will not offer you a position. But many of my own transactions are in need of new direction, and can always use new capital. If it is a question of investing money—"

"I am afraid it is rather a question of realizing on some existing assets. Assets which are far from liquid, but which may be made very profitable."

"I see." Warren paused for Franz to give a fuller explanation. There was silence.

Warren cleared his throat. He took up his glass and came around again to the front of the bar. "I wonder if we shouldn't be getting back upstairs. I should like to introduce you to—"

Franz gestured to the prone form of Charles. "I am afraid I have a responsibility here. May I join you in a few moments?"

Warren trotted unevenly away. Franz stood quietly in front of Charles, sipping his drink. Better to let him rest for a minute.

"Oh!" Nicole was at the door. She had been crying.

"It will be all right, Nicole," Franz said softly.

Her face grew stern. She came into the room and looked with little pity down at Charles. "I cried when Linda told me. Why did I cry? Perhaps only from humiliation."

"Too much is being made of this small unfortunate occurrence."

She shook her head angrily. "It is the latest of a series. There is now an intriguing topic of discussion in Westmount: what is it best to do with Charles Porter-Smythe when he is passed out."

He touched her arm. "Let him sleep for a little while. We will find it easy to waken him. Come, let's get away from here."

"Oh," she said again. Oh, I cannot bear it at all, she said within herself, but the words could not form themselves before Franz. She would not look up to his face, but her arm continued to rest in his hand. Slowly she felt herself turning to him.

"It is not possible that"—she began the sentence passionately but when she lifted her head to meet his eyes, the speech died. She came into his arms, and more, she came with her body entirely to his whole body, until they were together as one. Her lips were on his lips, her mouth was his mouth, there was a surge of pounding tension, there was an absence of all time. The months of dull frustration, the nights and nights alone, the lack of any release, of any satisfaction, any honest love… She came to her senses and fought against him, fought against this vice, this deadly sin. And Franz released her.

He spoke, in a voice that could not be calm. "You want me. More than I want you, you want me."

"No. No. I"—her voice was low-pitched and denied her words. "No. I—cannot. I cannot want you."

And she was gone.

Charles Porter-Smythe lay prone. His eyes were closed. His breathing was quiet and peaceful.

Scene Four

Cameron got on to Information. After a few minutes, he got Franz Loebek's number and called it.

An urbane voice answered, "Mr. Loebek's apartment."

"My God!" said Willie, shocked, "Who are you?"

"Whom were you calling, please?"

"Franz. Franz Loebek."

"And who is calling, please?"

"Who is answering?"

"This is Mr. Loebek's man, Marius."

"Well, hoo-ray for you," Willie chortled. "Tell the mastah Willie Cameron wishes to talk with him, will you?"

After a minute Franz came on the line. "Willie?" he asked. "You're two days late."

"Sorry. I was busy spending Morrie's ch
               eque."

"I thought you had perhaps become frightened again. I was preparing to go ahead without you."

"Well, things have been simplified for you. Now you can go ahead with me. What do I do?"

"Have you a key to the gambling house?"

"Sure."

"It has been closed since Morrie's death. You had better go and inspect it. Also, can you round up a staff?"

"If we're not in cahoots with Beaumage, all I can get is amateurs. But I know some pretty fair ones."

"Then contact them. And call me back before dinner tonight, to tell me how things have progressed."

"I may have to flash a small roll here and there. And I don't have too many bills to flash, right now."

"Call me back. We'll arrange a meeting."

"Where are you?"

"I will tell you. But now, go to work. The time is ripe to begin this operation. Call me." He hung up.

Willie sniffed. "The time is ripe," he mimicked. "Huh. I hope Beaumage is on a long vacation."

He got up from the bed, and a wave of nausea struck him. He went slowly to the bureau, got the glass and bottle, and came back to the bed. A little while later, he remembered to call the valet and send his new suit out to be quickly pressed. He called room service as well, ordered a T-bone steak, a double helping of ice cream and a large pot of coffee, and ate well when these came. By that time it was four o'clock and his suit had been returned.

He dressed in a violet shirt, a pink-and-lilac horror of a tie, and the suit, which was a Lower East Side tartan. He eased his swollen feet into pointed blood-red shoes, went out and locked the door behind him.

There was a brief pause in the flossy bar of the hotel, where he drank two martinis to clear his head, and a second bottle to take with him to the club. Then he hailed a taxi and said, "Six-twenty LaGarde Street. That's two blocks east of Papineau and just above Ontario, and go right there because I'm not a tourist."

He sat back, a little hungover still, a little drunk, at peace with his inner qualms, and enjoyed the ride. The driver sped along broad West Sherbrooke, threaded through the maze of East Sherbrooke Street traffic when the road became mean and narrow. Then the cabbie turned down LaGarde and stopped just in front of the old dark house.

It was a house of grey stone, a little alien to its setting. Most of the houses up and down the street were identical. They were four-family dwellings, curved iron stairways leading to the second storey flats in the style that persists for block after block in Montreal's east end.

The house rose two storeys from the street with a dormered third floor. It was old and grimy, and a plumb-bob would likely have shown its walls out of true. Black shutters were closed across the windows of the ground floor. Three broad, worn stone steps led to a vast, black front door.

Willie paid off the cabbie and stood for a minute on the sidewalk. He felt as if spying eyes were upon him. The street seemed alien and unfriendly, not the quiet neutral setting of the club he had known in earlier days.

All he really needed, he convinced himself, was another drink. He shrugged, fished for a key, and went to the front door of the old house.

As soon as he crossed the threshold, his footsteps were hushed. The floors were carpeted on the ground floor, in every room, from wall to wall. It was very dark. He went to a switch by the gaming room entrance, but it did not work. The power had been cut off at the main switch.

There was a flashlight in a place he knew. He went to the closet under the front stairs, groped and came out with a torch that gave welcome light. Only then could he begin his inspection. Into the gaming room he went, a room that had been formed by knocking together three rooms of the ground floor. In its L-shaped expanse he saw the three roulette wheels, the four card tables, the two dice tables. Nothing had been touched, not even the dust-covers over the equipment.

He went on to the small cubicle at the back of the gaming room that had been Morrie Winter's office. Here he set the flashlight base-upwards on the desk, so that its pale light travelled in a cone to the ceiling, formed there a circle of moonlight-yellow illumination, and reflected about the room. He unwrapped the bottle he had been carrying, found glasses and a decanter in a cabinet at the side of the desk, and made a trip to the little lavatory opening off the office to fill the decanter with water.

He sat at the desk, and squinting at the glass in the dim light of the torch, poured himself a drink and splashed water in it. He took the telephone from its cradle, and heard the dial-tone as he put it to his ear. At least it was working.

He lit a cigarette, and used the match flame to illuminate the telephone more brightly so he could see to dial. "Give me Joey Corner," he said into the mouthpiece. "Joey, it's Willie Cameron. You working these days? Well, how'd you like a night job too? No, no, easy. Run a crap table for me. Got a little place just opening up. Going to start any day now. Oh, sure, we're lousy with protection. Anyhow, you get paid in advance. Twenty-five bucks a night, all the time you stay honest... Okay? Swell. Go order yourself a new tux tomorrow; this is a class joint. I'll come around and see ya with some mazuma."

He hung up, drank, put his cigarette butt on the rug and scuffed it out. He drummed his fingers on the desk and tried to think of a good English roulette croupier; he was determined he would hire no French-Canadians. Finally he lit another cigarette and using the match as before, began to dial again. He had dialed three digits when a faint noise caught his ears and he stared up.

The ascetic face was poised like a mask against the cone of pale light. "Please," Rosaire Beaumage said, "go ahead. I did not mean to interrupt."

Willie's wooden fingers dropped the phone back on its cradle.

"What do you want?"

Willie had not intended to whisper, but the words came from his throat in a harsh, near-noiseless croak.

"Ah, Willie, I only wondered what did *you* want. You see, we keep close watch. We wonder who wants the old club closed—and why. It does not seem too sensible that Morrie should speak from beyond the grave and close it down, the old club. Morrie was always a friend to me. He did not do this thing, did he?"

Willie shrugged. "I dunno. What are you talking about?"

"The club. It is closed."

"Yeah, I heard. So I—"

"It was closed by Morrie's orders, so his lawyer said. But I cannot see—Morrie was not vindictive." Rosaire Beaumage paused. He went on with a fierce intensity, "*Why are you here?*"

"Like I said, I heard the place was closed. I come around. I wanted to look at it, for old time's sake, like."

Rosaire shook his head sadly. He sat heavily down in the padded chair fronting on Morrie Winter's old desk. "You should not have come, Willie. It was not for that, but even for that you should not have come." He indicated Willie's bottle. "I will have a drink."

Cameron poured the drink with shaking hands. "Water?" Rosaire nodded, and he added water from the decanter.

Willie said with slight bravado, "Why shouldn't I have come? What's wrong with that?"

"You are supposed to be far from Montreal. You know that."

"Whadda you care if I stay here? So long's I keep my nose clean, I—"

"But so hard," Rosaire said pityingly. "So hard to keep your nose clean, Willie, you know. You're such a snivelling creature. Nose always dripping. It cannot ever be really clean. Take the matter of Joey Corner."

"I don't—"

"Of course you know what I mean. You just called Joey and offered him a job. Naturally, Joey checked with my boys."

"Look, Rosaire—"

"Mister Beaumage."

"I guess I got suckered into something." Willie spoke very rapidly, his words tumbling. "I guess I didn't know how wrong I was in this. All that happened, a guy phoned me and said he was going to open up this house again and would I get some operators for him. I told him I couldn't go back in the business—because you didn't want me to, you know. And he said that was all right. I was just to set the house up again for him. And I asked him was it cleared with you. Of course it was, he said."

"This man is—?"

"A friend of Morrie Winter's."

"His name?"

"He wouldn't tell me his name."

"You were a fool to go into this, don't you think?"

"Well, now you make me see it that way, Rosaire. I guess I didn't realize. You mean," Willie asked innocently, "he was doing this illegal? He hadn't checked with you?"

Rosaire rose from the chair easily, almost indolently. His hand slashed out and struck Willie full on the mouth with the force of a hurled stone. There was a large diamond ring on Rosaire's hand and it left a mark above Willie's lips that turned red, and after a moment purple, and then began to bleed. "Do not take *me* for such a fool," Rosaire said, and slowly sat again.

They were silent for a while.

Willie said, "I'll go. I'll leave town tonight."

"It is too late."

"What do you want me for? What can I tell you?"

"Think of all the things you have not told me. Most of them I already know. But tell me them. I will know when you lie."

Willie began talking rapidly again. "There was this guy, see. He was Morrie's friend—no, really, Morrie's nephew. I think he came from the States somewhere. Name was Carl Winter. Morrie told him to carry on the house, and told him about me. He found me in a bar. I was just trying to raise a stake to get out of town, then I would've gone, right off. But he said he needed me. I told him. I told him you didn't want me here in the game any more, he should carry on without me. He said he was going to square himself with you, and he'd square me too. He told me to go ahead."

What made him loyal to Franz Loebek? Why had he hidden that name? Willie didn't quite know. Perhaps the apprehensive feeling that it would be worse to have Franz angry with him than to lie to Rosaire; perhaps just the tendency of the beaten man to tell as little as possible while still providing a credible story. In any case, the story seemed this time to satisfy Rosaire.

"What was the man's name?"

"Carl Winter."

"And he was Morrie's nephew?"

"I think so. I don't really know. I didn't hear from him until after Morrie was dead."

"How did he propose to operate this house?"

"Just in the old way, I guess. He wanted me to get operators for all the old equipment. He said he had plenty of money to finance an opening stake and we'd start right away."

"Did he say where he got the money?"

"No."

"Did he say how he would square you with me?"

"No. He only promised he would. Otherwise I never would've come near the place," Willie said piously.

"I see." Rosaire drained his glass and set it down. "We need another drink."

"Sure." Willie tipped the bottle.

"You too," Rosaire gestured. "And we need more water."

Willie trotted to the lavatory and refilled the decanter. He came back and watered Rosaire's drink, and his own.

"Here is to Carl Winter." They raised their glasses and drank; Willie drank very deeply before lowering the glass again.

"Then—Carl Winter is square with you?" Willie asked it anxiously. There was no Carl Winter. There was no one square with Beaumage, as far as this house was concerned. But he was deep in his own make-believe.

Rosaire said almost kindly, "That does not matter, Willie. Not to you. The important thing is, you are square with me."

"Honest?" Willie swallowed. His throat felt dry. He took another deep gulp of his drink.

"Yes, we are all square now. Let me tell you about yourself, Willie. Let me tell you things about you, some that you know, some that you have not known.

"You were born in a slum off of Jarvis Street in Toronto in 1916. You were the son of a sloven mother and of a father who had been fighting in Europe two years before you were born, and who luckily never came back from the war. All that is true."

Willie nodded.

There was a kindly, soft expression in Rosaire's usually frigid blue eyes. "I do not blame you for hating, when you came from that, Willie. You had to find someone to hate. You could have hated negroes or Jews or Catholics. I wish you had chosen to do that. But you chose to hate French-Canadians. When you had come to Montreal and had a little authority, a small bit of power, you showed that very clearly. And, Willie, I do not allow anyone to hate my race. Not if it's possible for me to prevent that."

Rosaire stood. "Well, I am going."

"But—you said we were square."

"We are, Willie. Stay here quietly. And I would advise you not to smoke; the place might catch fire when your cigarette dropped down."

"What—?"

"A little medicine, Willie. In the drink. Tasteless, when dissolved in alcohol. It was a sensible way for you to commit suicide." Rosaire picked up his own glass to take with him.

Willie opened his mouth to scream but no sound passed his throat. Suddenly, a great wave of muscular constriction engulfed his whole body. It passed, a giant tremor of controlled twitching, up his trunk, to his shoulders, to his head. The head swung instantly without his volition far to the left, cracking with a loud noise against the back of the chair. His mouth lolled open, the tongue falling down from it and little drips of spittle drooling toward the floor.

His eyes were open, staring. And his eyes saw.

Rosaire stepped into their field of vision and looked carefully, kindly at him.

"I wonder what Mr. Carl Winter will think?" he mused; and left the room.

Willie could not move. He had no consciousness of breathing, but his life ran on for a moment more.

My body. What will become of my body?

To hell with my body. Mother of God, my soul, my

soul. There is no priest, there will be no priest in time.

He thought to shrive himself and from the sorry welter of his sins picked the most recent: the drunkenness of the night before, the woman who had stayed with him. A woman of Sodom, of Gomorrah, of abominations... But what abominations! No part of his mind, not the memory nor yet the sensual part, had yet died and he thought longingly of her and of the things they had done alone, and did not ask again to be forgiven.

And then the quick poison crept further into his nervous system. It touched a ganglion below the brain and his breathing failed. The last air he would ever know rattled from his lungs, his vision blackened, his consciousness failed, and he dimly thought at last: God damn Franz Loebek.

Scene Five

"Marius? That you?"

"Yes, sir. Who is calling?"

"It's Franz. Are you sober?"

"I am broke, Excellency. So far as I can discover there is no liquor in the house—unless it is hidden with diabolical cunning. I am sober."

"I need you."

The grimness of his tone silenced Marius. "Yes?"

"I must rely on your discretion and your judgement. I hope you will be equal to this."

"You sound as though you have killed someone."

"Probably I have. Will you come?"

"Of course."

"Call Grand Radio Cabs and get driver six-thirteen to pick you up. Come to number 620 LaGarde Street. The front door of the house is in darkness, but the door is open. Have the driver wait for you and come in."

"Right."

Franz hung up the telephone and sat before Morrie Winter's desk. He held the flashlight for a moment on the frozen form of Willie Cameron, and then with a grimace switched it off. A moment later he rose, directed the beam of light before his feet and went from the office, through the gaming room into the front corridor. He cast the beam about until it rested on a closed door, which he opened. It revealed a broom closet. He closed the door and looked further until he found another door leading to the cellar stairwell. Here he found the main power switch of the house, and when he locked its bars in place the rooms above burned with light.

He went back and sat down again opposite Willie Cameron. The office light had come on with the others. He could not take his eyes off Willie. He was sitting there when Marius found him.

Marius said nothing for a minute. He walked gently around Willie's form. He looked intently into the open eyes and smelt the sagging mouth. Finally he looked at Franz and asked, "How did it happen?"

"I don't know. I sent him here."

"He was poisoned. I suppose by something in his drink; I can only smell alcohol. Have you called the police?"

"No. I cannot bring myself to call them if there is another way."

"You had better explain. I don't understand."

"This was Willie Cameron. I told him to come here and call me, later, for instructions. When I telephoned you at six he had not called. I became worried. I drove here."

"How did you get in?"

"The door was unlocked. He was here. I have touched nothing in this room."

"Why should we not call the police?"

Franz gestured to the gaming room. Marius went outside. He prowled around and looked under several dust-covers. Returning, he said, "So this is the source of your great wealth."

"If it were I should know exactly what to do. Probably I should have assistants older and more familiar than you. No, it is merely that I expected this to be the source of my future wealth."

"Just a minute." Marius went to the doorway, and immediately returned. "I have made sure the cab will wait. Now I must know the whole story."

"Before the police are called?"

"Clearly, it can make no difference to Willie."

Franz told of Winter, of Winter's death, of the legacy. He explained his acceptance of the house only on the basis that he needed funds to live as he wished.

"And Willie?" Marius asked.

"He was Winter's croupier. I needed him to start the operation of the house again. I persuaded him against his better judgement to come with me, by appealing to his greed."

"Against his better judgement?"

"There is supposed to be a gambler king of Montreal, named Beaumage. No house can operate without his blessing, but I proposed to cross him. And Willie Cameron was a man he had dismissed from the gambling business, perhaps because of personal dislike. I said I would protect Willie. I—did not keep my word."

"You appealed to Willie's greed. Let us examine my greed."

"What do you suggest?"

"It is not a question of what I suggest, but of what you are suggesting. Your own thoughts are clear. Willie must not be found here by the police, for the place would then be closed. Willie must be removed. After that, however, you are faced with the problem of operating the place. I have some knowledge of such things."

Franz gestured at Cameron's contorted body. "As much knowledge as Willie?"

"That does not frighten me. This Beaumage can have no personal distaste for me, since he has never met me. We will arrange a settlement with him, I will take over management of the house, and you—"

"No. We will come to no terms with Beaumage."

"Then you have a choice. You abandon the project or resign yourself to sitting, someday soon, where this body sits now. I wish you good fortune before that happens."

"We must fight Beaumage."

"You may fight him. I find poison distasteful."

"I had a plan. It has not worked. Approached more carefully, it would work a second time." He told Marius of his idea to bewilder Beaumage, to stay constantly as a guest in the house and intervene only if trouble arose; to stay the hand of Beaumage until it became too late for him to strike.

"It is a fine theory," Marius agreed.

"You believe it might be workable?"

"Yes, I am often crazy enough to believe in logical dreams. With Willie out of the way, it might work. But I see no point in such a scheme. There is great risk. And it would be simple to take out an insurance policy, a policy on our lives. If we insured with Beaumage I cannot think the cost would be great."

"Our independence. It is not the tribute we would pay to Beaumage that disturbs me; it is the whole idea of Beaumage. You expect me to be sitting where Willie sits. I would see Rosaire Beaumage there."

"The tarnish begins to rub from your shining armour, my knight. We are not going into business only to keep our penthouse fed and clothed. We are about to rid Montreal of the dragon Beaumage. Come, is he that bad?"

Franz let Marius follow his gaze to Cameron's body. "This is an example. For no valid reason—just a whim. And I know of worse examples."

"We may ourselves become worse examples."

"Oh, leave! I must decide what to do. You are of no assistance at all. I would have been better advised merely to call Jules."

"Who is Jules?"

"The cab driver. Outside."

"You know him? You trust him?"

"As well as I know and trust you."

"Then one problem is simplified. We have a third conspirator… In passing, I am still curious to know what bait you offered Willie."

"Twenty percent of the profits."

"Not enough. It is far from a major consideration. But that is not enough."

"I would expect more of you than Willie. I would offer you twenty-five percent."

"Ah, we enter upon a new relationship, Count Franz."

"As you say, Prince Marius."

"No longer master and man, except when others find us together at the penthouse. That should not be often."

"You will not go on living there?"

"I cannot persuade myself I should sleep here. The place might attract Rosaire's unsavory attentions at some lonely hour. So—I will stay at the penthouse, but I must become an invisible man there. There must be no further public connection between us, or you will lose your value as a shill."

"A shill?"

"Shill: at a carnival, the first one to play a game of chance. Usually allowed to win, thus encouraging the others to play. Of course, the shill is a member of the firm."

"I see. You plan to use me as a shill."

"You had planned that yourself, you know. You must tell your friends I left your employment because a more interesting opportunity came my way. That can explain your knowledge of this house to bring them to. I will use the service elevator to the penthouse, and the back door. I will not answer the telephone, unless you let it ring seven times, hang up and then immediately call again. We will manage."

"We have not begun to manage. There is still Willie."

"I can take care of Willie."

"How?"

"I have no intention of telling you. Help me."

Together they lifted Cameron's form from the chair. His body was not entirely rigid, and straightened as they lifted him between them. They came to the front door. The street was dark and deserted except for the cab of Jules Trebonne, which stood directly before them.

Marius looked at Franz. "Leave the liquor in plain view. I shall want a few good drinks when I get home." He called out, "Jules! In order to retain your innocence—close your eyes!"

FOUR

Scene One

Charles Porter-Smythe sat spraddled in a chair with his thin legs askew and his head turned sharply left, talking to the girl Annette who sat beside him. He grinned in amusement at something she said, grinned showing his teeth parted and his tongue protruding slightly between them.

He was not Charles at all, but Willie Cameron.

Franz squeezed shut his eyes in a grimace resembling weariness, but privately of fear. He opened them again, and of course it was Charles he saw. But for a flash, from a trick of light, a trick of posture, Willie Cameron had been able to haunt him again. Willie came to him sometimes when he was trying to sleep. Willie came to him in dreams more vivid than those he had after shooting down German planes.

It was silly. Willie had died, his body had been moved, his body had been found the morning after he died. His body had suffered no indignities. And there was no reason, Franz told himself over and over, to assume responsibility for his death. Willie had taken his chances with his eyes open.

But I said I would protect him. I promised.

There was the ghost of Willie and the living presence of Marius; hard to say which disturbed him more. Things had not turned out as they should have. Despite the way he was disquieted by the memory of Willie, he wished he himself had disposed of the body. Marius, in doing that, had found his first source of power over Franz. And then, how the man had changed!

Marius had been sodden with drink for two days after disposing of Willie. He had come home that night to drink all the liquor in the penthouse; in the morning he had demanded money, which Franz could not bring himself to refuse. He had returned the following day, slept fourteen hours, and had not tipped a bottle since.

This weak, ambitionless wanderer, this soft, alcoholic hulk had become a bustling man of enterprise. He had flown to Toronto, made a lightning raid on clubs there and returned bringing ten experienced men. There were two box-men for the craps tables who had started their gaming careers in Chicago, a poker house-man and a blackjack dealer from Reno; one of the roulette croupiers he had found even had brief Monte Carlo experience. How this congregation had been garnered from Toronto could never have been explained satisfactorily to most natives of that city.

The success of his expedition had given Marius a new idea for strategy in the fight with Beaumage. "We will all be from Toronto," he explained to Franz. "We represent an invasion of Montreal by big Toronto gambling interests. Rosaire knows the reputation of those gangs. He will not want open war with them. He may take our presence as a challenge and marshall forces to strike, but he will not risk a battle for the sake of wiping out one small operation."

The suggestion had merit, Franz realized. Marius was slowly taking the initiative from him. He was left with leadership only in the later matter of carrying the fight to Beaumage and destroying him.

Franz reviewed his adventure in Montreal. He could have refused Morrie's offer and stayed at the Chatham; but already that seemed unthinkable. On finding Willie, he could have walked out of the LaGarde Street house forever and gone to work for Warren, or Porter-Smythe, or one of a dozen others; but Willie's death had provided another reason for struggling against Rosaire. Lastly, instead of calling for Marius, he could have taken Willie away by himself; but with Willie gone he needed another associate, and Marius was the only person to call. He had misjudged Marius, but he could regain mastery over the man.

The speculation was all fruitless. He was committed to his path. Temporarily, as with many men of action, his burst of activity in moving from the Chatham and setting up his penthouse establishment, had been followed by a period of lethargy and doubt. Into this action-vacuum Marius had stepped to keep the project moving. But now it was his turn to act again, and this evening would see the next step.

A man, a friend of Bill Gladwin's, approached him and spoke jovially. "Franz, I'd like some lessons on how to be a perfect host."

Franz smiled, bowed a little and shrugged.

"I'm not kidding. I don't know how to do it. There are parties that rocket along from the sheer explosive force of the quantity of alcohol served. There are parties all loused up with charades and guessing games and cute ideas for drawing people out, where the extroverts have a hell of a time and the introverts laugh their poor heads off and then go home and drink laudanum to forget. But you have some perfect method. You appear to let each one do exactly what he wants, and yet with little nudges here and there you turn the whole thing into a roaring success."

"I enjoy entertaining so sincerely that I cannot allow anyone to have an unhappy evening."

"And how do you arrange that?"

Franz laughed. "Confidentially, I take great care not to invite anyone who is likely to be unhappy." The man grinned and moved away. In a sense, Franz thought comfortably, that was right. This gathering was no rolling crystal goblet, shooting sparks. It was smaller and more intimate than great cocktail parties of the Warren type. The people here all knew each other, most of them had known each other for years. There was no obvious strain between them, no unusual artificiality or striving to maintain face or conform to a common gay pattern. It was a comfortable party, like a low, glowing fire that Franz prodded now and again to bring forth a shooting little flame of laughter.

He went to the self-service bar he had set up on a long table at one side of the grey and scarlet room. He mixed rye and water, and turned with his glass in hand to look about the room. Inevitably, the first person to catch his eye was Linda.

She stood with a small cluster of men about her, and beyond the men a fringe of attendant women. Even the women seemed not displeased to form her audience. As a night-club entertainer sings with her body, as a burlesque queen dances with her body, Linda talked with her body. Out of range of her voice, one could imagine the story she was telling—probably a most innocent tale—to be one of the more intimate episodes of the *Decameron*. An upward thrust of her breasts, a wide sway of her hips, a lazy, sensuous caress of her hands down her curved body, illustrated the anecdote. She did everything but pull the zipper of her sheath-tight dark green gown, a gown that descended from two thread-like shoulder straps in a manner more daring, more exciting than could be achieved with any strapless model. She was not talking; she was performing.

Of course, she knew Franz was watching her.

His gaze left her and fell on Nicole. The girl stood with a small group—Gladwin, another couple—before the fireplace. As he looked she bent her head and with a curious intentness kicked slowly at a small ember that had sparked out from the fire. It was a lithe, easy, completely unselfconscious movement of her long slim leg under the full skirt of her red gown. She was lost in her little preoccupation, deaf to conversation, dreaming with unhappy eyes her sorry thoughts.

Franz thought, no, he knew that he could let Linda give herself to him, that he would take her with a fierce elation. But the woman he wanted, wanted forever, was this natural, this utterly beautiful girl. She was a woman to sleep with then wake up with, warmly close in the chill of morning. She was a woman for play, for laughter; for understanding, for tenderness; for joy, for sweet passion. If he could only bring her to his arms again as she had come that once...

Bill Gladwin caught his eye, then left the group and came toward him. "Well, Franz."

"Bill, your glass is empty."

"So is my pocketbook."

"Your—?"

"Kidding, just kidding. But I've been wondering about my investment. Ten thou is ten thou. Besides, I'm incurably curious. How's the enterprise been going?"

"There was a slight delay."

"Oh?" Gladwin let a shadow of a frown cloud his face.

"It has been overcome. I must not make rash predictions, but I think we may have some dividends tomorrow. I will be calling you."

"You still can't tell me about the project?"

"I am afraid I must be secretive for a long time. In fact, you are likely to guess before I tell you. There is an exception to this, though. If your dividends are not regular and satisfactory, you will receive full details."

"I'll be patient." He went to rescue Annette from Charles.

Linda bore down upon Franz. "They tell me you're living in this gorgeous penthouse now."

She came toward him as she spoke, walking like a woman of Babylon. He said, "Yes, don't you like the decor? It was personally chosen by Le Comte de Maligne."

"What happened to Le Compte? He was a pet."

"Alas, his creditors discovered he had no more hard currency. He has gone where francs are legal tender."

"This isn't what I really wanted to talk about at all."

"Then why not say what you wished?" Franz looked at her and was amazed at the depth of expression of which her dark eyes were capable. She was a brown-eyed blonde, a girl with such deeply pigmented skin and brown-black eyes that her hair must surely be bleached; and then you looked at the hair and it gave you the lie to that thought. It was long and lustrous, smooth and strong, strong as the form of her face. She had a straight nose, a long jaw that gave her face shape and kept it from beauty, and expressed in physical terms the uncompromising nature of her spoiled soul.

She said, "I wished to admit I have been a stinker. I tend to be a stinker. Many people love me for it. But I don't mean to be, and I'm sorry."

"Don't mention it. I think nothing of it," Franz said pleasantly. "I expect you to be a stinker."

"I set that reporter, Burns, on your trail."

"Of course, you admitted that to me."

"And I was damned mad when he didn't splash your picture all over his paper," she said, adopting the utterly frank approach. "I wanted to embarrass you. Or something. I wanted to do something to you. I still do."

"Swing your hips again. That does something to me."

"I'll slap you. Right here."

"Go ahead. It will mean a lot less trouble in the long run."

"I see what you mean. All right, I won't slap you. But I'm lying in wait."

Franz presented her with the hint of a formal bow. "It is a delightful thought. I shall watch carefully for you in my moments of weakness."

"Do you get weak often, Squadron-Leader?"

"Why not steal away, go into my bedroom, and wait? I will be there in time. I am at my weakest when tired."

Linda slapped him resoundingly. Then she laughed.

She called to the assembly, "It wasn't as bad as it sounded. But, girls, don't let him tell you any jokes."

She went away, still making a good show of laughing.

There was a pause in which he merely surveyed the party, satisfied that it was running smoothly, wondering how he might uproot and transplant them to the gambling club. Then he caught his breath.

Nicole came toward him, quietly and smoothly as

though on tip-toe. The soft red gown flowed back from her body as she walked, outlining the beautiful shape of her. Her black hair was parted geometrically in the center of her head tonight, and caught at the nape to train it down her back in a flowing stream. She had no colour but the vivid slash of red across her lips, and her olive face had an undercast of paleness. She looked up at him and the whole world of their love was in her eyes; she could prevent everything else, but not that. She offered her firm, slim hand, looking down.

"We must go. Thank you for the wonderful evening."

"But the evening has not begun."

"We must go. You need not ask why."

He saw from the corner of his eye Charles sprawled sloppily in a chair, eyes squinted, mouth writhing as he tried to talk.

He held her hand. The pressure was a little more firm, more intimate than either willed. "Do not go."

"You see we must."

"I have something in mind. Something more exciting than mere drinking, something that will change the whole tenor of this party. Wait ten minutes. You will see."

She drew away, doubtfully.

He raised his voice enough to stop all other conversation. "A tragic thing has happened!"

Voices cried, "What?"

"You see," his arm swept across the bar, "the bottles have emptied themselves. We must move on."

"My place next," someone called.

"I have a great idea." He came across the room to the others, and they gathered to him. "You remember my man-servant Marius? No? I was blessed with him for a few days. Then he left me to return to his main occupation. He is the manager of a house where one may risk one's luck. Have we all white ties and long dresses? Good, then we may all go there. I will regard it as an insult if anyone refuses. Marius has promised to let me win one hundred dollars for each thousand any of you loses."

Thus the voice of the shill in action. And there were squeals of delight and murmurs of approval. A voice: "Is there barbotte?"

"No, no. Did I not say white ties?"

And a doubter: "This is a square house?"

"If not, you may complain to me."

They all without exception went with him.

Scene Two

Linda called above the jabber of sound, "Franz! Come here and explain roulette to me."

"I am engaged. I will send Marius, he can tell you far more than I."

He pressed toward the dice table which was getting heavy play. His party had scattered about the big game room of the LaGarde Street house. There were no others there. The party occupied one roulette wheel, one card table, one dice table.

The reopened house had an air of opulence and pleasant, non-deadly sin. The game room was well but softly lighted, the lighting fixtures all concealed in the wainscoting. Dark oak panelled the walls, and the wall-to-wall carpeting was of a blue so deep as to become almost black under the lights. The game operators were formally dressed, courteous and quiet, and the hand-picked guests were behaving themselves in an awed, unfamiliar way. They had gambled before, but their gambling had been done in great draughty barns where noisy French-Canadians played emotional barbotte at a dozen tables, or in hideaway hotel rooms where crap games operated with a minimum of equipment, or in the old days in the grand gambling places of Montreal where hundreds mingled and your closest neighbor might be a hard-faced gunman with a bulge under his arm, and a cold fishy eye on your first suspicious move.

As Franz moved toward the crap table Gladwin caught

his arm. "Say, I think this is a sucker trap you've steered us into."

"Oh, come! If it is, we will know soon."

"Know what I bet that guy Marius does? I bet he goes around from place to place, staying a few days and planting the idea this is a good place to come to. You notice the joint was empty when we came in? I didn't like that. Neither did a lot of the others."

"Marius said the place was just opening."

"Did he say to come this particular night? Is that what he told you?"

"Well—he did say that it would open this evening."

"Uh-huh. I thought so."

"I will stay," Franz said firmly, "until I am convinced something is wrong. And I am not inexperienced in these games. But if you, or someone else, sees a crooked deal, come to me. I feel a responsibility. I will make sure the right thing is done."

"Okay. But I'm going to stop drinking right now."

Franz found Charles Porter-Smythe clinging to the crap table. It was a long, wide, baize-covered table bigger than the kind used for table tennis, marked off in the intricate betting pattern adopted for "house" crap games. Charles, his eyes half-glazed, obviously could not make head nor tail of it.

"Wha' they playing?" he asked Franz thickly.

"Crap."

"Nonshence. Played crap. Y' throw dice on th' floor."

"This is a house crap game."

"Wha' you mean?" Charles fixed his eyes on Franz. They seemed clear.

"You always bet against the house."

"Heh." Charles looked smug, as though he had unexpectedly found himself very clever. "I know better than that. Bet the dice to win all the time, dice are loaded to lose, nobody wins but the house."

"In a house game, you may also bet against the dice.

See, in those squares on the table."

"Oh." Charles was shaken.

"The different squares represent the kind of bet you make. You put your stake on the square you choose, as in roulette. You may bet a certain number will come up, that the roller will natural or crap, or simply that he will win or lose his point. There are odds on all these bets that give a slight margin of profit to the house, according to the laws of chance. But the game is honest. See," Franz pointed, "the box-man is giving dice to a new roller. He offers him a container with six dice, and the roller chooses any two he wishes."

"Who's a box-man?"

"He stands there in the centre of the table, with a long crook to pull back the dice. He is the only person besides the roller who may touch the dice. He controls the box, where the house keeps its money, and he umpires the game. There are also two end-men, at either end of the table. They accept bets, pay off bets."

"You play an' show me how," Charles begged.

"I was going to play roulette, but—I'll stake a bit here. We'd better go to the other end of the table. This is the fifty-dollar end, and my chips are twenties."

"No, stay here. I've only got fifties."

Franz shrugged. They crowded to the margin of the table.

When the dice came to him, Franz laid five twenties on "win" and five more on "natural" to provide Charles with a good example. He chose his dice and rolled nervously, praying for at least an easy point.

The dice showed seven.

He passed the dice to Charles. "See? You take these while they're hot. I only wished to show you." He went back to inspire play at the roulette wheel.

Charles looked at the dice for a minute as they lay in his hand. The box-man fidgeted. Charles fumbled them and one fell to the floor. An end-man swooped for it, returned it to the cage on the table, and the box-man shoved the cage to Charles with his crook, chanting, "Choose your dice, please, let's get on with the play. Place your bets, gentlemen, dice coming out. Choose your dice, sir."

Charles sniffed in annoyance. "That was the hot pair!" He chose a second die at random from the cage and with a petulant flick of his hand threw ten fifty-dollar chips on the "win" square.

He shook the dice and threw them to the far end of the table. They rattled against the board.

"Big dick. Ten it is, ten to come," cried the box-man, sweeping the dice back to Charles with his long crook.

"I can make ten," Charles said belligerently. "I always make ten." He threw two more fifties to fall on the ten square at the center of the table.

He threw again and again. His face flushed. He threw an eight, then a six, then a nine. He threw a final time, rubbing the dice between the palms of his open hands to warm them before he rolled.

"The hard way," the box-man called, "five and five, the hard way, big dick, place your bets, gentlemen, dice coming out."

The end-man gave Charles a stack of ten to match the ten he had to place on the "win" square. The box-man placed a high pile of chips beside the two he had bet on ten and shoved them to him.

"All that?" Charles asked, eyes sparkling.

"The house pays fair odds, sir."

"I feel a natural coming," Charles said, and put ten chips on that square as well as ten on "win."

He rolled eleven.

Franz came back to the crap table an hour later to watch the play. In the few minutes he was there Charles took the roll, made a six-point then an eight-point, naturalled, crapped, made little Joe and crapped out on a nine. The pile of chips before him was impressive.

The change in Charles was also impressive. The mist

had left his eyes and he wore an expression of fascinated glee. He rolled the dice accurately, without fumbling, and his bets seemed sensible and practised.

Nicole came and stood in front of Franz, not noticing him as she watched her husband. Franz let her follow his play for a minute and then said quietly over her shoulder, "You see? He is not drinking."

She turned and regarded him soberly. "No," she said flatly.

Charles noticed them and called, "Franz, Franz, look! I've won ten thousand dollars!"

Franz shuddered.

Scene Three

The day after the club opened, Franz slept until noon. He had been too tired, perhaps too apprehensive, to await Marius' return from the club the night before. He woke with a feeling of worry that puzzled him until he remembered its origin. He padded in bare feet to rouse Marius.

Marius snored. He lay fully clothed on his narrow bed in the little servant's room. Franz stubbed his toe on an empty whisky bottle that lay on its side just out of reach of the man's dangling hand.

Marius took a great deal of waking. He also took two cups of black coffee before he could talk sensibly. Franz made the coffee, dressed while Marius was drinking it, and then came back to the room. "Well?" he asked.

"I drank nothing, nothing at all until the club was closed. And I will be in perfectly good condition to go there again tonight."

"I do not question that. I am not concerned with how you feel. What happened to the club?"

"Nothing had happened to the club when I left."

"I mean the play, fool. What did we win or lose?"

"Oh, that." Marius yawned, and covered his mouth

with his hand while his stomach rattled volubly. "Well, we did not pay off the customers with the chips. For a time I thought we might be reduced to that."

"I saw they were paid in cash. But what is our own position today?"

"I expect we have nearly a thousand dollars of the original stake. Let me see, we began last night with something over five thousand of the ten thousand you first gave me—the rest has gone on expenses and advances to the men. We paid out four thousand, two hundred twenty dollars cash. Quite a bit of it to the women, luckily, which is very good advertising."

"Then we have not enough to play tonight!"

"Ah, and whose fault is that? You brought a wealthy crowd to the house. You did not limit the play."

Franz was silent. I cannot go to Gladwin again, he thought. Could I go to...

"Of course," Marius reached into his breast pocket, "there are these." He thrust a wad of cheques to Franz. "I don't know whether they're worth anything."

Franz riffled through the cheques. There were about a dozen, ranging in amount from fifty dollars to six hundred. They totalled more than three thousand dollars. "This is better," he grunted.

"And here's something." Marius drew another cheque from his side pocket." What do you want to do with this?"

Franz looked, and could hardly believe it. Charles Porter-Smythe had signed a cheque for eighteen thousand dollars.

After a moment it was Marius' turn to ask, "Well?"

The door buzzer rang.

"Close this door before you answer the bell," Marius said sharply. "I'll go out the back way later. What about that cheque?"

Franz flung it at him. "Cash it," he said harshly. "He's good for it."

Franz opened the door wide, and the man, without a word, walked in. He looked about appreciatively. He said, "'S wrong? Servants' day off?"

He was short and chubby. He had a wide-brimmed fedora, which he had not removed. He wore an overcoat tailored for a man eight inches taller and sixty pounds heavier. He had a plump, rounded, rather fatuous face in which no feature was outstanding, and the heavy horn-rimmed glasses he wore achieved no effect at all, certainly not the impressiveness he aimed at.

"You can't live in a place like this and answer the door yourself, you know," he said.

"What do you—?" Franz began, and suddenly stopped, recognizing the man. It was Burns, the *Clarion* reporter.

"You skipped out on me," Burns accused him.

"Ah, I am sorry. You are right. I am afraid I forgot."

"You left no forwarding address at your rooming house. No forwarding address at the Chatham Hotel. Were you trying to duck me, perhaps?"

"I was trying to duck everyone."

"Then you should have had your new telephone listed under someone else's name. The press is resourceful, you know. We think of things like calling Information."

"Of course, of course. I am exaggerating. I was not really trying to duck people, nor hide. I only cut my connections with my old life, and began a new one."

"Fine. What's it all about?"

"All about?"

"This new life. Come on, remember me? I wanted to do a story about you. I agreed to wait a week, wait for a better story. I trusted you, I wouldn't have waited for any other reason."

"Of course. Well, your story. What do you want to know?"

Burns sighed deeply. "I see how the press rates, here. We don't get invited in to sit down, or anything. We get talked into standing in the vestibule, like we were—"

"Come in, come in." Franz led the way to the great drawing-room with grey walls, the scarlet drapes, the broad fireplace.

Burns sat in the middle of the chesterfield, and spread out his huge coat; it enveloped the chesterfield. "I want a story," he said simply.

"Ask your questions."

"How did you get this?"

"Money. How else?"

"Do I gotta be coy? How did you get the money?"

"I used my credit. Very uninteresting. No angle to it at all. Nothing that would make a story."

"What have you done recently," Burns asked, "that *would* make a story?"

"Isn't that up to you?"

"I need co-operation."

"Burns, you were all set to feature me as a head-waiter with a glamorous past. That would have made a great story, eh? Providing I was an aspiring, enterprising head-waiter—or would pretend to be one. I'm afraid you've lost that story—or at least, I'd rather you didn't print my experiences at the Chatham. So, I suppose it's up to me to give you a better story than that."

"You promised to."

"I don't quite know how to do it. You'll have to find your own angle. I have simply changed from unenterprising waiter to enterprising businessman—but there is nothing duller than a businessman, is there?"

"Nothing I can think of," Burns said glumly. "But maybe I can dope out an angle. You got any beer here? Oh, no, never mind. Someone's waiting for me in the car. What kind of business?"

"Just managing some investments—my own. I haven't an office, or anything like that."

"What kind of investments—stocks and bonds, real estate, grocery stores—what?"

"Real estate."

"Who set you up in business?"

"I acquired some friends."

"You're being a lot of help."

"You know what businessmen are like—business secrets, and all that. I'm afraid I can't really tell."

"Did Morrie Winter leave you his money?"

Franz was startled, but showed this only by a slight hesitation. "Why would you ask that?"

"You didn't save enough money, working at the Chatham to nthouse and buy real

eone. He had no close And he was a good iged the funeral." Suppose the funds I Europe? Naturally, I Or, suppose one of —had provided me by revealing that."

r, it would be a The will would be

"The will wouldn't be probated for a while, and I want to write a story this afternoon."

"You have not brought a photographer."

"I'm going to use one of your wartime portraits, from the morgue. More glamorous. You don't deny Morrie left you your stake?"

"I'll sue you if you print that."

Burns grinned. "Oh, I won't. I'm just curious. I know lots more than I print."

"Have you found your angle yet?"

"There isn't any angle. Just another routine story. Tell me, Mr. Loebek, why did you decide to settle in Montreal?"

"I came here directly from Europe. I liked the city and decided not to move on. I find the people friendly and hospitable."

"Now there's a quote for me." Burns made a great play of getting out his notebook and pencil. "Friendly and hospitable. I'll use that. Have you any other thoughts?"

"Nothing printable."

"Don't be huffy. I might write about your Chatham episode."

Franz flushed. "Write about it then, and be damned."

"I was only kidding, I'm always kidding. I can see you're not one to kow-tow to the press."

"Nor to anyone, Mr. Burns."

"Bully for you," said Burns. He stood, his oversize coat swirled about him. "You know, I have a feeling that when I learn some more about you, you'll be very interesting. I won't learn it from you, I'm afraid. But I'll find out. Goodbye for now. Watch for the morning *Clarion*."

Scene Five

Marius locked the evening's proceeds in the safe at the back of the house and came through the ground floor to the front door, turning off the lights one by one as he proceeded.

The guests had gone, Franz had gone, the operators had gone. Nothing was left in the house but Marius and thirty-three thousand odd dollars in a fireproof, burglar-proof safe; and a collection of cloth-covered wheels and tables that stirred men's blood and overcame their prudence—brought their wallets out, their money down on green baize squares; brought them gain or loss, elation or disgust... and by the inexorable laws of chance poured a steady dribble, a fixed, honourable percentage, into the house safe.

Good business.

Marius laughed to himself. Good business—his business. Twenty-five percent! Soon he would force Franz to make him a full partner, for Franz could not operate this club without him. And later…

For a homeless wanderer, an habitual sot, a man who had never held a job nor a friend nor an unspent dollar, this was an unbelievable sinecure. It could not be denied that he had the upper hand on Franz; and would use that advantage, for he felt no obligation, no loyalty. Franz was playing a wicked game, and deserved what was going to happen to him.

Marius was in the vestibule. He put his hand on the knob of the coat-room door but did not open it. Instead, he went into the small bar opposite the entrance to the game-room. He poured himself half a tumbler of Scotch, sat on a bar-stool, and took a long, fragrant cigar from an inner pocket of his tail coat. He took a long, slow swallow of the Scotch, a leisurely inhalation from the cigar, and mused.

Certainly Franz could be bested in this affair. And then, what of himself? He had no ambition to fight Rosaire Beaumage. This one house represented the limit of his desires; he could happily spend the rest of his life operating it.

Things had never been so good before. He thought of his past life, and sketched it in his mind in a series of phrases: the terror of revolution in his youth; the hopeless poverty of the landless refugee; the servility of his career as a waiter; the sodden degeneration of his drinking habit.

What will he had left was only directed to living, living in comfort until he died or whisky killed him. He would take this house from Franz, because Franz was dangerously amateur in his ideas about running it, dangerously vindictive against Rosaire Beaumage—and that could lead to loss of everything. It was necessary that Franz should go. He could look after himself.

There was a light knocking on the door of the house. Marius listened intently, but did not move. The knocking came again, and then he heard the front door open.

He dropped his cigar in an ash tray, slid his rounded fundament off the bar-stool, and hitched his shoulders to straighten his tail coat. He went into the vestibule.

Back to Marius, a quietly dressed man was gently shutting the front door. He turned. He was a young man, well-groomed. He wore a black fedora exactly flat on his head—the way, Marius thought, a priest wears his hat.

"Good evening," the young man said pleasantly. "You are Mr. Winter?"

"Good morning, rather than good evening," Marius said stiffly. "I am sorry, sir; this place is closed. The front door should be locked—someone was careless."

"Very careless, Mr. Winter," the young man agreed.

"I am not Mr. Winter. I am sorry to tell you that Mr. Winter is dead."

"One Mr. Winter is dead."

"I'm afraid I do not understand."

"Morris Winter is dead. You are perhaps his nephew, Carl Winter?"

"No, my name is Marius; I am the manager here."

"Your face is not familiar to me, Marius. And I expect you do not know me. Let me introduce myself—I am Rosaire Beaumage."

"Ah! Shall we go to the bar?" Marius asked. His only thought was that he must have another drink, quickly. His knees were rubbery, and he felt that everything—probably including his own life—depended on how well he could talk and act in the next few minutes. Outwardly, he bent every nerve to preserve an appearance of confidence and unconcern.

Rosaire refused a drink. Marius put a little ice in a fresh glass and again poured himself a drunkard's portion of Scotch. "Then the door *was* locked," he commented.

"Of course. The carelessness I agreed to was your own. It would have been only wise to change the lock."

"That could have but postponed this meeting." Marius took a long drink; he rested his glass on the bar, but took care not to take his hand from it. He said, "I have expected this encounter. It was inevitable. I have received instructions as to what I am to say to you. They make my position a most dangerous one, whether I meet you alone or accompanied by friends, by night or day. I am about to play a game of poker with you, Monsieur Beaumage—a hand of showdown. Shall I turn up the cards?"

"Please do so."

"First, an ace to you. You may dispose of me here and now—as you disposed of Willie Cameron."

Rosaire laughed. He did not bother to deny the charge. "And who would carry away your body, as you carried Willie's away from here?"

Marius said boldly, "A party of twenty or thirty men— or as many more as would be required to bury me and— investigate my death. They would come from Toronto." He paused. "An ace to me?" he asked.

Rosaire nodded his head gravely. "It is possible, I will not deny that. Perhaps we should cease our game and discuss this matter straightforwardly."

"It came to the attention of my Toronto employers that this house had been bereaved of its owner."

"Through information furnished by Carl Winter, the late Morris Winter's heir," Rosaire interrupted.

"Of course," Marius agreed.

"You see, I know much of this story. Go on."

"My Toronto employers decided that—"

"Who—Kaslik? Multo? Barrovitch?"

"Let us say Barrovitch, since it is not Barrovitch. Barrovitch, then, decided one small Montreal house would be profitable—at least, an interesting venture. He saw that this house was closed, and after a short time, sent me to Montreal to reopen it."

"You made a great mistake," Rosaire told him, "getting Willie Cameron to assist you."

"I see that now. And I apologise. I did not mean to offend you unnecessarily."

"Who found Willie's body?"

"I did."

Rosaire shook his head. "No, no. Remember, we were watching."

"Actually, a man blundered into the house and found the body. You left the door unlocked behind you. He was a wealthy man, one I expected to be a customer of the house. He confused the date, and arrived that night. After finding Willie, he called me. As you said, you were watching; you saw, then, that it was I who took away the body."

"Go on."

"After such an unfortunate experience, I returned to Toronto and brought a complete staff back with me from there. You can have no personal objection to them."

"Only to what they are doing."

"I will tell you how my—how Barrovitch has reasoned this. He is interested only in this one house in Montreal. He is not a foolish man; he would not attempt any large-scale invasion of this city, and invite a war with you. Similarly, he takes you for a wise man. He does not believe you would risk war with him to wipe out one small nuisance like this little house."

"He has reasoned well. But it is at best an unstable situation. Would it not be far better to come to an arrangement? I would be willing to consider most generous terms. Fifteen percent, shall we say?"

"I am but an employee. I shall certainly communicate with Barrovitch, and give him your view."

"How quickly can you do that?"

"It may take a little time."

"If it should take too long, I fear—"

"Monsieur Beaumage, surely nothing would happen to me? Nor to the house? No matter how accidental an occurrence, it is clear that Barrovitch could suspect only you."

"Perhaps I should risk that."

"I must take that chance, of course. When we began

this talk, I acknowledged that my position was most dangerous. I can only trust my poker sense."

"Are you sure you know when to withdraw from a hand?"

Marius drank deeply, and left the question unanswered.

"*Au revoir*, Marius," Rosaire said suddenly. "I will be back to try my luck. Perhaps you will have something to say to me when I come back again."

"I shall communicate with Barrovitch."

Rosaire smiled, and his rabbit-teeth glistened damply. "You must point out to him that this is most unfair. I have never tried to control a house in Toronto. I have no desire to do so. Perhaps I must risk war, just to keep my own city disciplined, unless Barrovitch will acknowledge my authority here. I am not sure. I must consider the problem. Meanwhile, of course, I guarantee you nothing—no protection. My protection is very valuable here; without it, many things might happen. You must conduct yourself with care, my friend. Good night."

Rosaire walked from the house.

Marius poured another drink.

Scene Six

Marius stumbled into his room and fell awkwardly on his bed. Franz heard the noise and went to the rear of the apartment, entered the man's room and turned on the light. What he saw was no pretty picture. Marius' eyes were glazed, his limbs twisted, his breathing stertorous.

"Where have you been drinking?" Franz asked sharply. "It is after five o'clock. You know I expect you to check in with me, at least by telephone, before this hour. I was beginning to be worried."

Marius bowed his head in mock submissiveness. "Accept my abject apologies, Excellency. I was delayed."

"By a fifth of Scotch."

"No, by something worthy of your worry."

"What happened? Come, man, come!" Franz shouted, for Marius' face had stiffened into an expression of staring idiocy.

He blinked his eyes and shook his head. "I have met the great Rosaire."

"What did you tell him?"

"The Toronto story."

"And his reaction?"

"I think I bluffed him. I may have bluffed him. But I am not really sure. It is like not being sure the revolver at one's head is really loaded."

"What did he say?"

"He demanded fifteen percent of the house from my Toronto employer. He will call back for an answer. If it is not soon in coming, he will not guarantee our safety."

"*Our* safety? Drunken fool, did you tell him my part in this thing?"

"I was not drunken then," Marius said with dignity. "No. I did not reveal you. It is really only I who am unsafe. I have no stomach for that. If the bluff seemed certain to work, I would be brave as you. But under the circumstances, it is necessary to give Rosaire his cut. I think we will have come off cheaply."

"We make no compromise with Rosaire. I have told you that."

"Then I withdraw."

"I had been meaning to appeal to your greed again," Franz said. "It seems the one method calculated to give results. I am prepared to offer you a danger bonus—a higher percentage of the receipts."

Marius began to laugh, his great larded body shaking. He laughed foolishly with the uninhibited laughter of the drunkard, tears springing to his eyes and saliva dropping from his lips. "You fool!" he said. "It is you who are the fool, not me. Do you not realize I was prepared to take over more of the receipts—no, the whole house!—when I was ready? You cannot run this house without me. Face reality. I will strike this bargain—"

"Stop this babbling!" Franz shouted. "And begin to pack."

Marius went on as though he had not been interrupted: "I will strike this bargain with you. I will accept my present share of profits, at least for a time. And we will pay Rosaire his fee. And I will stay."

Franz bent over the slumped figure. Both hands gripping Marius' lapels, he jerked him to a sitting position and held him strongly, roughly, the tail coat pulled half up his back.

"Have you never thought, Marius, that there might also be danger to me? Rosaire and I are in the same business just now, and I may have to adopt some of his methods. Perhaps not poison, but there are other ways than poison. Would you enjoy such a whipping as I could give you?"

He threw Marius back on the bed and the man lay gasping and rolling his eyes. Franz went on, "Perhaps you think me blind. But I have watched you change, Marius. I have followed your thoughts in the attitude you have adopted. I see you consider me now only your shill, a man to be retained in the business only so long as he is useful, and then pushed out of it. You cannot do that, Marius, Recall your own weaknesses, and ask yourself if you can deal with him when I am not behind you."

"I—will make my own peace with Rosaire!" Marius gasped.

"Do that, and be prepared to deal with me,"

"I will withdraw, then. Try to operate the house without my knowledge. You cannot do it."

"I have learned much recently. I should be glad to do it. You are welcome to leave. You may leave tonight."

Marius was still panting. "No, not tonight."

"Stay, then. And beginning tomorrow, we are again master and man. You will do what I say, you will run the house as I say. Moreover, Francis of the first roulette wheel will audit the receipts for me."

The door buzzer rang.

"I have been followed! It is Rosaire!"

Franz regarded him scornfully. "You need not be worried. You are safe in my care. Recall that, Marius. Take not a step out from my shadow."

Scene Seven

Franz opened the door and looked at Linda.

"What do you want?" he asked ungraciously.

"I couldn't sleep. The gambling was too exciting. Well, let me in."

"I am about to retire."

"Good then, you're weak," she said insolently. "Remember?" She swayed past him into the apartment. She was wearing the green gown she had worn to his evening party a few nights before, and a smooth beaver coat was thrown over her shoulders.

Franz followed her into the drawing-room. She paused in the center of the floor, turned and stood staring at him.

"Thirsty?" he asked. "Hungry?"

"No."

"Cigarette?"

"No."

"Then what is it you want?"

"You, I guess."

"There is a very broad choice available to you. Why should you want me?"

"I know *what* I want. Do I have to know why I want it?"

"You must know how to get it."

"I'm working on that."

"I'm afraid the play was not successful. Your father seems prepared to offer me a position, but it does not interest me."

"I'm making another play."

"It is too obvious."

"I don't know that it is. Why don't you want me?"

"Why *do* you want me?"

"You're strong, you know how to get things you want. I like men so strong I have to force them to want me."

"Nonsense. You know nothing about me. I appeal to you physically, that's all. Perhaps there is someone else who appeals to me the same way."

"Is that what love is?"

"Of course. What else?"

She shrugged off the beaver coat and let it fall to the floor. She might have been naked, for all the concealment the green gown afforded. "Who is more appealing than I am?"

"Perhaps a girl with crossed eyes. Each has his own tastes."

"I didn't need to ask. I know what you want. Well, give up. Nicole is married. Nicole is a Catholic, and practically medieval about her religion. The only way you could get her is to kill Charles."

"Perhaps I shall."

"God, we're strong tonight. I'll have that cigarette now."

"When I am ready to give it to you. Do we stand here like this the rest of the night, facing each other like fencers? Sit!"

"I don't choose to sit. I won't do anything you say. God, we'll be good together!"

"Your reasoning is ridiculous. We would be abominable together. We would fight day and night."

"Hate and love are close."

"So it has been said. I prefer a love without the tinge of hatred."

"You'll die without stimulation."

"I am not a man to be whipped to action, nor a horse to be ridden. I need no companion with spurs."

"I say you do. I would devote my life to raking your sides with the rowels. I would make you a great man."

"I prefer to be a happy, satisfied man."

"You will never be satisfied if you refuse me. You'll always wonder what I would have been like, if you passed me by only because you were afraid, afraid I might conquer you."

"I could take you and then toss you aside. Have you thought of that?"

"No man could ever toss me aside."

"You are too young to know the truth of things. Anyone can be tossed aside. All that you have said of me is more true of yourself. You will not be satisfied if you do not conquer me, so you come whoring to me in this sleek green gown, thinking to suck me to you. Beware. You are in far greater danger than I."

"Give me a cigarette."

"Come to me and get one."

He drew a silver case from his breast pocket. She looked at it an instant, and then looked in his eyes again. "I want you!" she said passionately.

"You want me to rule, and break, and throw away. That is all you will ever want of men. You have no feeling but for yourself, Linda. And I value myself above you."

"You're missing a great experience," she said. "I've been told that. You know something? I'm not one of your svelte, frightened, purebred Anglo-Saxon beauties from a tired old Westmount family. I'm a slum kid. C.C. was lonely, and he had his housekeeper adopt me. I don't know where I came from, but the families that threw me up were full of liquid fire. Maybe I'm part Negro; sometimes I think I smell Negro. I'm basic. I don't care for anything but food, heat in winter, sun in summer. And men. I need men. Strong men. Are you strong enough for me?"

"You throw out a great deal of sex. And nothing else."

"What did you just say? What else is love, Franz?"

She came toward him. "Cigarette."

He opened the case and held it to her. His other hand brought out a lighter.

Linda slapped him with all her strength, full across the face. He showed no reaction. She slapped him again.

"Well, drop your cigarettes and hold me. Or laugh at me, I don't care. Do something. Do something!" she almost screamed.

She struck him again, this time with her fingers curled, the long nails raking his cheek and almost immediately drawing blood.

Franz threw the cigarette case to the floor and seized her hands. He shook her. "Stop this frenzy!"

"The green gown. I saw before that you liked the green."

"Yes."

"I was not wearing it at the gambling house tonight. I wonder if you noticed? I went home to change before I came here. Look at the straps, Franz. They're so fragile."

He threw her away from him. "You may go."

"Look at the straps, Franz. They'd be easy for a strong man like you to tear away. You know something? Or had you guessed? Look at me Franz, there's nothing under the dress."

He looked at her body.

"You can see me so much better without this useless thing. Tear it off. Or will I shame you and tear it away myself?"

Franz shook his head slowly. In two steps he was upon her. "This is your doing."

She laughed excitedly. "But not my undoing. Not my undoing!"

He put both hands over her full breasts, at the bodice of the dress. Without effort, he ripped the gown apart and it fell to the floor.

Linda's body was all it had promised, clothed.

She pressed herself to him. "Take me to bed, Franz. Take me to bed!"

He threw her roughly to the rug. "You were not made to be taken in a bed," he said harshly.

FIVE

Scene One

"I take it all back," Bill Gladwin said. "Now, I'm convinced. This is a square house, all right. And very well run, too."

Franz smiled. "You must have won money."

"No, I've lost. But not more than I could afford, and I've had a very fair shake for my cash. Good fun and good diversion. I like this place. You're always here, Franz, you seem to have given it some of the atmosphere of your own parties. I notice the rest of the crowd likes it too. Can't walk in without stumbling over Porter-Smythe, or Winslow, Carswell or one of my other ne'er-do-well friends."

"Then you have lost your suspicion that Marius planted himself with me to entice the crowd here."

"Yes, because it's square. And for another reason—if he were using you, he'd be damned careful how he behaved toward you. He isn't."

"What do you mean?"

"I don't like the way he stares at you. Have you had a fight with him over something?"

"You are very keen tonight, Bill. Yes, as a matter of fact we did have a quarrel. Not a serious matter."

"What?"

"Not a serious thing, really nothing."

"Boy, you are crawling with mystery. Why? You make a mystery of a simple thing like that. You make a mystery of my investment—won't tell me what you've done with my money. It was quite a bit of money—ten thousand dollars. So three days ago you give me ten thousand dollars back—and say it's just a dividend. A dividend! What have you been doing—gambling on some good penny mining stocks?"

"No, not that."

"What, then?"

"My dear Bill, you are asking very dangerous questions. Do you remember the old fable of the goose who laid the golden egg?"

"Implying that there may be more dividends if I restrain my curiosity, none at all if I'm too inquisitive."

"Quite. But don't say, 'There *may* be more dividends.' There are more dividends, already. So sit back trustingly and enjoy your profit."

"I shall, I shall. I've got to leave now. Are you staying?"

"Yes, for a while. Why leave so quickly?"

"Because of that," Gladwin said, looking toward the first dice table—at Charles Porter-Smythe.

They watched in silence for a minute. They were close enough to see the play.

Charles was playing at the fifty-dollar end of the table, as usual. The dice came to him. He shoved two stacks of fifties, representing one thousand dollars, onto "win," and rolled. He crapped with snake-eyes, and the end-man drew in his chips.

One thousand dollars.

Charles pushed two more stacks of the chips onto the table. He rolled again. The dice came up two and two— Little Joe. Charles rolled the dice again, again, again. They rolled high—eight, eleven, six, nine, ten—seven.

Two thousand dollars—lost in minutes.

Charles shrugged, and smiled. It seemed as if the loss was meaningless to him. Quite possibly he had been drinking heavily before he began to play; his little chin sagged slightly, and though his eyes were clear and followed the play keenly, he squinted them with the effort of focussing exactly. His sparse, sandy hair was dishevelled and small areas of pink scalp showed between its clumped strands. There was a smudge of black dirt on his white tie.

But he belied his appearance with an air of studied calm, the insouciance of the gambling habitué. He, Charles, was now a man among men; a gambler, a good fellow willing to risk a thousand on the turn of the dice. How the others must envy his daring, his steeled nerves!

One who did not envy him was Franz, who had kept a running total of Charles' losses and found them approaching the fantastic total of one hundred thousand dollars in the few weeks the house had been opened. Charles had been supporting the house almost single-handed; it really needed no other customers. How long, Franz wondered, could his madness keep on?

And Gladwin was not deceived. "We should have our heads read for ever bringing Charles here. With anyone as neurotic, unstable and dull as him, we might have known what would happen. I consider it's partly on my head, and I'm getting him out of here before he loses his shirt."

"He already has," Franz commented. "I've seen one or two of the cheques he's been signing at the end of the evening."

"It's utter foolishness. His net income can't be more than forty or fifty thousand a year, and I'll bet he's dropped that much in the last few weeks."

"It would not surprise me," Franz agreed.

"After that, he can only dip into capital. His capital is his firm, and it won't stand too much dipping. Well, here goes. I'll try to pry him away. Lend me some support if I have trouble, will you?"

"Certainly," said Franz, but immediately got away to the far side of the room and became absorbed in roulette.

"Charles!"

"Oh, hello, Bill. Have you been watching? Those dice are cold as an evening in Nome, tonight."

"Good time to leave them alone. Let's get out of here and come back again. I'm just going back to my place. Come along and have a night-cap."

"Thanks all the same, old chap, I've become very pure. Sworn off drinking before breakfast. Besides, I need a few rolls here to even up. Always have one streak of real luck in a session, you know. Haven't had it yet, this time."

"Haven't you dropped enough for tonight?"

"Don't be silly. I've dropped too much. Have to stay, absolutely have to."

"Where's Nicole?"

"Home in bed, I expect. We had a short altercation about whether we should come here, and compromised. I came."

"Charles, you're a fool to buck this run of bad luck you've been having. A professional gambler would tell you that. And you're only a novice at the game. You're being taken, Charles, taken. You have no sense about betting, even I can tell—"

"Why, how should I bet, Bill?" Charles asked. His voice was quiet, but there was submerged rage in it. He did not look at Bill; he watched the play as a man at the far end of the table rolled and rolled vainly for a point.

"Bet to minimize your losses and maximize your winnings. It isn't hard, but there's a knack you have to learn. I learned it in friendly games where I couldn't drop more than a few hundred dollars—a month's Air Force pay. And you've got to learn it pretty quickly, Charles. Or you'll be ruined. On the street."

Charles looked at him. The anger left him, and to Bill his tone seemed only pathetic. "Would that matter?"

"Things are never so bad," Bill said brusquely, "that you can't make them worse by being a damned fool. Now come on, let's leave. And give this business some thought before you come back here again."

Charles was very earnest. "But you're wrong, Bill, if you think I'm not learning. I'm losing less every night. In a little while, you watch, I'll begin to make real killings. Then see if you still think I'm a novice!"

"Fine. But tonight, as a favour to me, quit it."

"Oh—all right. But I owe the house six thousand. Damn."

Charles fumbled in his pockets and brought out a chequebook and a pen. He filled in the cheque and called, "Marius!"

The broad, bald man came to him and bowed. "Yes, sir?"

"Here's the damage for tonight. I'm afraid I've lost track of my bank balance, though; if it's not covered, hold it, will you? I'll fix it with you the next time I come in."

Marius asked obsequiously, "Could you give me a cheque on another account, Mr. Porter-Smythe? I'm sorry, I regret to have to mention this to you, but your cheque from two evenings ago has been returned."

"The devil! How much?"

"It was for twelve thousand, sir. And the cheque from last night, it may be that it will be returned—only two thousand. With tonight's loss, a total of twenty thousand dollars. If you would only tell me, sir, that you will make some arrangement, no more need to be said at all. I am sorry—"

"Of course I'll make an arrangement. A settlement. It may take a—a few days."

"You realize my position, sir. I find it most embarrassing to insist on a rapid settlement, but we pay out such sums each night that our assets must always be completely liquid. If you—?"

"I'll take care of it tomorrow."

"I knew you would see my point. Thank you very much. And I trust your luck will take a great change."

"Oh, come on, you don't really."

"I do, sir. The house, of course, always wins. But it is most disagreeable to win always from one client. The laws of chance ensure our profit, in exchange for the entertainment we provide. The losses, preferably, are spread widely,"

"Well, thank you, Marius."

"Thank you, sir."

There was a sharp call from the far end of the room:

"Marius!" He turned. Franz was beckoning him.

He bowed to Gladwin and Charles. "Pardon me, gentlemen."

"Yes, we're going," Charles said. "Come on, Bill. Good night." They moved toward the door.

Marius trotted to the roulette table. Franz eyed him sternly.

"Marius—what's wrong with this wheel? It has come double-zero three times in the last seven spins."

Marius shrugged. The eyes of all the others around the tables were on him, he noted. He said, "I am sorry, sir. But there can be no question regarding the wheel. It is of the finest quality, absolutely true. And as for trickery, if anyone here would like to examine it—"

"Things can be done to a wheel that no ordinary examination will reveal!" Franz said significantly.

Marius reddened. "You question the honesty of the house, sir. I will show you that it cannot be questioned. Jacques!"—he turned to the croupier—"Repay the house winnings from the last seven plays. Each player is to tell you his loss, and you will return the chips to him. Then remove this wheel, and set up in its place the spare from the cabinet in the basement."

"Thank you, Marius," Franz said stiffly. "You restore my faith."

Marius bowed. Then he turned and bowed again to the murmur of happy approval that rose from the players at the table. He went on his way around the room.

What had frightened Franz? he wondered. Had someone suspected his connection with the house, or had he himself suspected? In any case, he felt the scene had been brilliantly played on both sides. Franz was well cleared—as was the house.

A woman was entering the vestibule, a beautiful woman dusted with the light snow that had been falling throughout the evening. She was an unusual woman, Marius thought, to have been walking alone in her evening gown and wrap, with a film of shawl over her head, down dark LaGarde Street at this hour. The usual woman of her class would have hesitated to walk down LaGarde in bright daylight.

"Madame." He bowed. The doorman closed the great planked portal behind her, and Marius himself took her cloak and shawl. She was a lithe, live creature, he thought. Her white gown had been designed for her by a wizard—it was demure, but so daringly demure! And above the gown, above the winsome white shoulders, her black hair severely drawn back revealed the pure, oval beauty of her face.

"Madame is to meet a gentleman here?"

She was about to speak, when Franz approached them.

"Nicole!" he said happily. "It is good to see you. Charles was here, but he has gone."

"Oh, I am glad. I had come to—"

"Bill Gladwin persuaded him to leave, not ten minutes ago. Do you wish to stay? Or may I be allowed to escort you to your home?"

"I will go, Franz. But there is no need for you to come—only call me a taxi, if you will."

"Nonsense. One minute, while I pay my honourable debt."

He drew Marius aside, and brought out his wallet as he talked. "It is necessary that I leave you here alone for the rest of this night. Nothing can happen. Rosaire has not called back to inquire of our decision, and if he comes it will be only for that."

"However—if he comes—I may be unable to put him off."

"You will do that easily, in one way. Be bold. Relay to him, from Toronto, a series of realistic threats. Beaumage is a coward." Franz turned, took Nicole's cloak, and went to her.

A coward? Then what may I call myself? Marius thought.

Scene Two

There was a time in Linda Warren's past which now she seldom consciously recalled. It was a time when dirt and stale, rank smells had been normal, and cleanliness something to be avoided; when sometimes in the winter she was cold because the relief coupons had been traded for gin instead of coal, and often she had gone hungry after she threw her plate of greasy food onto the floor.

That was the time when she had learned how to use her feet to fight, and how to poke with a stick—poke at the attacker's face, at his eyes, instead of vainly, feebly beating him. It was then she learned small boys were Indians who wanted to tie you up and leave you to howl in the dark, or shove you down banks, or even, if they had a match, set your long hair on fire. And some men, too, liked to give candy to a little girl and talk softly to her, and then they wanted to play, and there was only one way to stop their frightening play: you kicked them hard, right between the legs, and ran a long, long way away.

Then the old man had gone away, or maybe he'd got drunk and fallen in the St. Lawrence. And Mom took her to a Home. It was a Home where they made you wash, and walk in a straight line with a lot of other girls, and they taught you things. Mom never came back to see her. Mom probably had died or got herself killed.

There was a day when all the girls in the Home were scrubbed and dressed in new uniforms, and lined up in the Assembly Hall. Then Miss Lemon-Puss came walking along the lines of girls, and with her was a little, round, waddling man with glasses that made his eyes look as big as all the rest of his face. The man stopped in front of Linda. He put his hand under her firm chin and lifted her face to his. "You're going to be a pretty girl when you grow up, a very pretty girl," he had said.

"Leave me alone!" Linda cried, and had lashed out with her foot. She'd kicked between his legs and almost hit the right spot, too, but he had jumped back.

He turned to Miss Lemon-Puss. "Has anyone offered to adopt this little girl?"

"No, sir."

"Bring her back to the office with us. She has enough spirit to live in my house."

That was how she became Linda Warren.

And what was so good about being Linda Warren?

You had soft, clean, pretty-coloured clothes, and anything you wanted to eat. You had a machine in the bathroom that spat water down on top of you and made it fun to take a bath. You had Mrs. Scittanelli, who was your adopted mother and never talked too much and never hit you except in self-defence. And, as the years went by, you discovered what power you had over boys because you were so strong and so attractive to them and so bold and teasing with them; and because C.C. Warren was your father.

Boys, and then men.

But not all men.

And Linda watched Franz take Nicole out of the La-Garde Street house, and her lips drew back in something that might have been a sneer but was more likely a snarl.

She thought of a tearing, throbbing ecstasy like nothing else she had ever experienced. And then pulling about her the shreds of her green dress, and pulling on her beaver coat, and driving slowly home.

Since then, she had not seen Franz alone.

One sentence he had spoken went over, over, over in her mind: *I could take you, and then toss you away.*

Oh, he was a fool, she would break him, she would bring him grovelling to her, she would frustrate him, she would kill him! He and his little snotty Nicole. They were a pair for you! Full of the serious sadness of life, full of sighs and unspent passion, massive problems and regrets. Nicole, calm, deep little bitch with her utterly worthless Charles and her stupid code that tied her to him. Franz would soon get tired of chasing a shadow. But—would he come back to her, Linda?

Tonight he had barely spoken to her. She had been playing the second roulette table; he had chosen the first. She watched him intensely, long enough to know he was avoiding her glance, was careful not to look her way.

With a fierce, loose motion she threw all her remaining chips on the red. The croupier chanted his little formula, the wheel spun and the ivory ball rattled about its rim. The black came up.

She turned and walked away from the table, swinging her evening bag slowly out and against her thigh, out and against her thigh. Jack Winslow, who had brought her to the house, called, "Hey, wait! I'm not through. Come on back, I'll give you some more chips." She paid him no attention. She simply left.

Scene Three

Nicole stood at the far end of the grey-and-scarlet drawing-room, looking through the French doors and down on the lighted city. "You should not have brought me here," she said. "More than that. Of course, I should not have come."

Franz lit a cigarette. He stood some distance from her, at the fireplace. "At least, we can talk alone. We have had no chance for that."

"And is that good? Or will it but make us more sad?"

"Anyone is sometimes forced to do things he knows will be saddening. Satisfaction can be obtained only at the cost of pain."

"Ah, we are being for too tragic, far too heroic," she said impatiently.

"Far too heroic," Franz agreed.

She turned from the window, but still did not look at him. She walked slowly, gracefully toward a table and took a cigarette. "I do not like it here. It is too high up."

"No higher than your own home."

"No, but there is a difference. This place is on a level

with the peaks of Westmount and Mount Royal, but it is high in the building—so high. The foundations are really between two mountains."

"Perhaps there is a significance to that," Franz said lightly. "I am on the Côte des Neiges, the pass between the two hills. I am neither on the one nor the other, but—"

"Between the two mountains. It might have a good or a bad meaning, you know."

"Of what are you thinking?"

"It is too hard for me to express what I mean," she said, frowning. "Besides, I do not know you well enough."

"You know all you need to know of me, as I of you."

"That means nothing."

"You are not in love with Charles."

"I agree. It does not simplify anything."

"And you are in love with me."

"You are so sure of that? You are more sure than I."

"You want me."

"And that is love?"

"It has a great deal to do with love, at least. Without it, there is no love."

"I believe that is how I made my mistake. I was not thinking so much of love, as of marriage."

"Why?"

"Oh, come! You are European. You know what is traditional and accepted as the procedure for a respectable girl, everywhere but on the North American continent. She must be concerned not primarily with love, but with marriage to a man of whom her parents approve. If he is physically attractive, if love can be developed, all to the good. But in the absence of love there is the marriage, the approval of the parents, security, care, a good home…"

"And this is true everywhere except on this continent."

"You should realize that French Canada is more a part of Europe, in many ways, than of North America."

"Yet exposed to both influences."

"Yes, and I more than most people of my race. You know something of my life? My father was wealthy, and enough of a realist to believe the English would always be the powerful race in this country. Our home life was traditional French-Canadian, but we lived in Westmount; all of our friends were English. They were English Catholics, preferably, but many were not even of our own religion. We had few French friends. Our schooling was in English."

"Yet your ideas—for instance, your idea of marriage—remained typically French?"

"There was my mother."

Franz took a step toward her, and took her hands in his. "And your ideas are unchanged? Any marriage—even a bad marriage—is sacred?"

She looked up to his eyes. "Now you ask me not about my customs, but about my belief. My religion."

"There are annulments, even in your religion."

"Not after the consummation of a marriage." She laughed. "I wonder if it could really be said our marriage was consumated, except by Charles? But, no"—she blushed and looked down. "I must not talk like this, with this frankness, even to you. I embarrass myself. Nothing, nothing can come of all this."

"You fear only that nothing good can come of it."

"Nothing can come of it at all." She stood on tip-toe and kissed him lightly on the cheek. "We must be friends, Franz. We could be great friends. There's so much more to our desire for each other than the basic physical—physical thing. There is an understanding and a perception of each other that is tender and knowing. An intuitive thing, because we have no deep experience or knowledge of each other. We can help each other much."

"No," Franz said bitterly, "you are wrong. We cannot be friends. We cannot help and understand each other— we cannot even see each other, if sleeping together would be such a terrible sin. Because 'the physical thing' would be there always, waiting to spring if we weakened. And then—because your background compels it—there would be just regret."

"They say the physical thing can be weakened, sub-limated. In good works, the Church says. Or in activity, in athletics—skiing. Do you not love to ski?"

"One can hardly ski all year around. And the physical side can be but weakened; it cannot be killed. When weak, it yet has more power than any other human desire."

"Then I have found no real solution, I suppose."

"None at all."

"Is there one?"

"Perhaps Charles may die," Franz said bitterly.

Nicole flushed. "It is unlikely. Now, I must go. Please take me down to the taxi stand, Franz."

Scene Four

Late morning.

Sun slanted against a high tower on St. James Street and knifed between the slats of Venetian blinds into a small office. A neat, bright blonde secretary sat where the sun's rays fell. She was worth watching, but Charles kept his eyes away from her. The radiance of her sunlit head was too much for his blurry vision to accept without protest, this morning.

The Colonel likes blondes, thought Charles. He likes that blonde daughter of his…

"Colonel Warren is free now," the girl said, alerted by a buzzer sounding softly somewhere in the region of her skirt. "Will you come in, please?"

She opened the door for him, and Charles walked into an office far smaller than his own. C.C. Warren believed in a tidy mind, a clean desk, and a spartan office. He had one telephone only and no intercom box. The desk was plain and the chairs were straight and severe. The carpet, Charles noted absently, was old, thin, even a little worn. But all these things were a deliberate underplaying of power and influence. Charles knew C.C. too well to let them breed a false sense of disdain. He felt, rather, like a young man applying for his first job.

"Morning, Colonel," he said, a bit diffidently.

"Good morning, Charles. Sorry I was busy when you came in. You should have phoned, you know. Not that I'm not glad to see you, but I have to run such a tight schedule here. Hated to keep you waiting. What's on your mind?"

"Ah—"

"Just one moment." Warren picked up his phone and ducked the other hand to a concealed push-button by his knees. "No calls for five minutes," he said into the telephone, "unless that call from Vancouver comes through. Busy." He cradled the phone. "Yes, Charles," he said pleasantly.

"I've been wondering if—that is, your advice. Had a little trouble lately, sir, and—"

"Your firm having a bit of a rough time? I wouldn't wonder. Some very keen competitors in that field. And, of course, in a one-man company like yours, if sales fall off you're for it. The liquid assets have to keep coming in, or the bills can't be paid, eh? Now if I were in your spot—"

"Sales are fine, sir. Matter of fact I brought the last quarter summary with me, if you want to see it later. This is more of a personal problem."

"Personal? But these are business hours, Charles."

"Well, personal in a way, but business in a way. Matter of fact…"

"Yes, yes?"

"Well, as I said, I'd like your advice, sir. The firm is about the only capital I have, as you know. Now, I seem to have run through my personal assets and I wondered if the firm could be—that is, if I wanted to realize on part of my interest in it, how should I go about it?"

"What's happened to your liquid assets? Steady drain

on them? Now that you're married, have your month-to-month expenses been higher than your income?"

"No, not at all. I've had some extraordinary expenses. I—"

"Been gambling?"

Charles looked up suddenly. "Why do you ask that?"

"I keep my eye on the market, naturally. Noticed the penny gold stocks fell right out of bed last week. Were you deep into one or two of 'em?"

"No, sir. Not that kind of gambling."

"Oh?"

"I mean—Well, I might as well come right out with it, since I'm asking you for—for advice. Real gambling, not the stock market."

"Real gambling? I thought that was confined to the French playing barbotte now, in Montreal. Where have you been going?"

"There's a house on LaGarde Street. Most of our crowd goes there, these evenings. Very posh—evening dress only. They have roulette, chemin-de-fer, crap tables."

"And what was your particular weakness?"

"Crap. It's an expensive game."

"And what is your problem?"

"I'm out of cash, that's all. And I owe twenty thousand which I promised to cough up today. I don't quite know how to get it, sir, to be frank."

"Well, you have an immediate problem, no doubt about it. No use talking about making your firm a public corporation and selling stock. That takes months. You need a loan. Bank loan."

"You think that's wise, sir?"

"To pay an obligation? Of course. It's always wise, if you can get a loan. And you'll have no trouble. Of course, you don't have to tell them you've been gambling."

"Of course not."

"If you want a long term solution, of course, I'm your man. You have a very good little corporation there.

I would take an interest in your corporation, willingly. Anything up to, say—five hundred thousand. That's all the cash I could really spare, in that direction."

"One hundred thousand was all I was thinking of, really."

"Well—"

"One hundred thousand for five percent of the capital stock."

"My dear boy, I would offer five hundred thousand for fifty-one percent of the stock. That means that for one hundred thousand I should have ten percent. But I'm not too interested in that, really. I'd be interested only in having some control over the firm, smartening up the plant operation and selling procedure—well, you know how I go to work on a business when I become really interested in it."

"Colonel, I don't want you to take over my firm. I wasn't suggesting that."

"An idea, though, isn't it? Look at my record for bucking up small companies, building them into large operations. Why, I can see such a future for Porter Bolt and Screw! And holding forty-nine percent of the stock, you'd profit as the firm grew."

"But it's ridiculous to talk of buying half the company for a half-million. Why, the net worth alone is over two million. I should be able to realize—"

"It's not what you can realize, Charles. If you want cash, cash of the order of one hundred thousand, you can't get that easily from the bank. You could get a substantial amount of cash from me—and the prospect of future profits matching those you get now from total ownership of the firm. Why don't you think it over? We could be fine partners."

"But wouldn't you like to take a small interest for—"

"No, Charles, I'm sorry. I don't work that way. A man has only so many hours. I like to keep personal watch on all my investments, and that isn't worthwhile unless I have a measure of control along with my interest."

"I see."

"You should have no trouble, if you go to a bank for twenty thousand. If you really feel you need one hundred, well—I don't know. I can't think of a good way for you to get it immediately. Of course I could give you far more than that, and all in the same day, if you want to consider my proposal. You'd better think about it."

"I will, sir. But I'd like to keep my business."

"Naturally, my boy. Naturally. It was your father's. But that's sentiment. If you think strictly on business lines and forget the sentiment, you'll see I'm right. Let me do all the work and I'll build a tremendous company there for you."

"No, for yourself."

"Only fifty-one percent for myself." Warren rose. "I hope you'll think about it. And if you decided in the negative, I hope your personal problems will straighten out in any case. Be more careful with that gambling. By the way, have you seen Linda in that LaGarde Street place?"

"Oh, yes. She's always there. Goodbye, sir."

"Good morning."

Charles left. Warren sat at his desk and fiddled with his push-buttons. He told the telephone, "Get me Garfield."

After a minute of listening he said, "Garfield? Warren. Fine, thank you. Yes, a job. There's a gambling house on LaGarde Street. I want to know all about it. Yes, everything."

SIX

Scene One

"Linda, will you be in for dinner this evening?"

She called through the closed bedroom door, "No Father, sorry. Got to go out."

"Well, I want to talk to you. May I come in?"

"Yes, of course."

C.C. Warren came into his daughter's bedroom and waited for her to emerge from her bathroom. The room received his disapproving glance. Linda was not neat, was not tidy, and even were the litter removed from the room he would not approve its furnishings or decorative scheme. He felt Linda had no taste. Her broad bed was a plain continental, without headboard or posts. The vanity, in contrast to the severity, was really antique, an old piece from his mother's home. The gold-coloured broadloom rug was too plain for the violently flowered window drapes, and the bedspread fought with both. The pictures about the walls were a tasteless mixture of sentimental prints, in large snapshots, and original oils that someone had told Linda to buy.

She came from her bathroom, wrapped carelessly in a huge terry towel. "Hello, father." She went to the chest of drawers, dropped the towel, and opening a drawer, pawed about for underthings.

"Linda!"

She turned, naked, and thinking nothing of her nakedness. "Yes, Father," she said impatiently. "I'm hurrying, I've got to go out."

"Do you have to parade around here in the nude when I'm trying to talk to you?"

"Well, you asked to come in. Really, you knew I—"

C.C. Warren was white with tension and hot with the passions he sublimated all day long in a spartan office, behind a clean desk which never held more than one telephone. His bug-eyes watched Linda, and wanted to look away, and could not look away. They took in every detail of her magnificent sexuality, the wide-spaced, up-tilted breasts with their prominent, dark nipples; the flat, hard belly; the flaring, flowering hips with...

"Oh, get into some clothes so I can talk to you."

Linda laughed. "I thought you could always talk." She turned back to the drawer, pulled out brief white silk panties and with easy, balanced swings of one, then the other leg, donned them. She took a wisp of a brassiere, swung in one shoulder and the second, and deftly hooked it behind her back. "All right, I'm presentable," she said. "You can look now. What's wrong?"

"What's wrong?"

"Certainly, something's disturbed you badly or you wouldn't come dashing in here. What is it?"

"You've been gambling."

"C.C., I should never underestimate you. I haven't been losing money. It doesn't show in my bank account. I've seen none of your friends in this gambling hell of mine. I've been the soul of discretion. But you know I've been gambling." She sat at the vanity in her underthings and began combing her long blonde hair softly, caressingly, as though that were the only important thing in the world.

"I know you've been gambling. And I don't like it."

She paused with comb in mid-air, caught his gaze in her mirror, and said petulantly, "Just why not?"

"This particular little place you've picked for your sport is a danger spot. There's going to be trouble there."

"What makes you think so?"

"When I found out you were going there I investigated it. I found some very interesting things. First of all, Rosaire Beaumage has not given it his approval."

"How did you find these things out?"

"Resourcefulness, my dear. How do you suppose I made all my money? Anyway, the point is that any place not approved by Beaumage is going to have trouble."

"Oh? What's so special about Beaumage?"

"I should think you'd know who he is."

"Oh, stop basking in your superior knowledge. Tell me who he is, and what's wrong with him."

"Well, to be brief—and unfortunately, I must use rather melodramatic language—Beaumage is the king of the Montreal underworld."

"No!"

"He's very sensitive about people starting gambling houses without his permission. That's why there's bound to be trouble at your place on LaGarde Street."

"You're thorough, Father, I'll say that for you. You even know where it is. What else do you know? Who runs it?"

"I'm still working on that question. There's a man named Marius—"

"I could have told you that."

"—who is the manager, but someone is behind him. I have some suspicions. Who first took you there?"

"I don't recall who—oh, there was a crowd of us. We were having a party at Franz Loebek's, and we all decided to go gambling."

"Who suggested the place on LaGarde Street?"

"I don't remember."

"Was it Loebek?"

"I don't remember. Yes, I think it was Franz. But that was natural; he had known Marius before the house had opened."

"I see."

"I wouldn't read too much into that, if I were you."

"You may remember that Mr. Loebek is so independent he won't even come to see me about a position, or even about investments."

"Well—"

"Are you still interested in him?"

"Oh, no," Linda said innocently. "Not nearly as much as I'm interested in Rosaire Beaumage."

"Ah, I think that's just wonderful," Warren said drily. "What would be more perfect than that you married, bringing him into the family. Together he and I would control all of Montreal."

"You're being so funny."

"I know better than to tell you not to see him. There's no easier way of driving you to him."

"How well you understand me, Father."

"Sometimes I wish I could understand you better. Or perhaps just wish I could influence you more."

"The most powerful man in the city, and he admits he can't control—"

"The most wilful daughter in the country," Warren interrupted.

"You asked for it."

"Don't be completely ungrateful."

"You asked for it, I didn't. Why I tried to kick you in the—"

"You and Rosaire would make a fine pair, I expect."

"Sure we would. Two children of the slums. Where did you come from, Father?"

"You know perfectly well."

"Of course, a poor but honest family. You walked five miles to school through the snow. Then you got a job at ten dollars a week, out of which you sent two to your parents and saved seven."

"You can sneer at things like that when you've tried to make a little money yourself."

"Father, you've made it unnecessary for me to earn any money. Don't expect me to appreciate your early struggles, please. Don't expect me ever to have any idea of the value of money. I have my own standards, but you've bred them in me."

Warren became angry. "I've bred some things into

you, but I've not been able to breed out the early influences, apparently. You've no idea of right or wrong—"

"Neither have you, you old pirate. Just what's legal and illegal."

"—Or of what's wise and what's unwise. I sometimes think you have no human emotions—"

"Except acquisitiveness. I know. A different kind from your acquisitiveness. I collect people where you collect corporations. I love my collecting as much as you love yours."

"Did you ever stop to think, young lady, that I have the final word? You were never legally adopted, you know, by me. You were adopted by that old fool of a housekeeper, and she's dead now. I could put you out without a cent."

"There are two things you may not have thought of. First, it wouldn't make the slightest difference to me. Can you imagine how many men would jump to marry me, or to support me without marriage? And also, I'd love to drag your name through the mud. You can imagine how it would sound to everyone: Yes, I hear Warren threw his daughter out on the street. Look what's become of her! Suppose the old man's off his rocker, doing a thing like that?"

Warren laughed. "That would please me immensely. Why, if people thought I was losing my mind, think of the deals I could make with the loony idiots who tried to take advantage of me!"

Scene Two

Beaumage lived and had his headquarters in an austere old mansion in Outrement, on the rear slope of Mount Royal, back from and high above a broad, busy street. He conducted much of his business here—Rosaire was not a man who went often to see others—and conducted it most often at night, since many of those he dealt with were not welcome in such a respectable neighbourhood in the daylight.

141

Rosaire lived and held court in a suite on the ground floor of the house. There was a huge office that had once been the drawing room of the home, still furnished more as a living-room than as an office. It had a long table placed athwart the high, narrow-paned triple window of the room, in such a position that Rosaire could sit behind the table without exposing his back to the window, and yet letting the light shine into the eyes of his visitors in daytime; at night, the illumination was arranged to give the same effect.

Tonight, Rosaire was holding court. And he smiled, almost laughed at the grotesque figure facing him under the glare of his lights. It was a short, plump, broad figure, dressed in evening clothes, and wearing a large, dirty burlap sack instead of a head.

Two men supported the figure's either arm. Rosaire said, "Remove the bag. Take it with you and go."

Marius was revealed. He was cowed. He looked about apprehensively, as if expecting to see a torture rack in some corner of the room. There was a jerkiness to his movements, and he had to make an obvious effort, swallowing thick saliva, before he could speak. "I do not understand this," he said. "Why have you brought me here?"

"I thought we should have another little talk. I did not wish to bother going to LaGarde Street, so I took the liberty of having you brought to me."

"Liberty! I thought I was being kidnapped!"

"Come, come, you haven't been mistreated. If you were frightened—well, perhaps that was what I intended, eh?"

Marius was silent.

"I realize this may mean some postponement of your plans to get to your place of work this evening. But you agree our business is most important—to you as well as to me?"

"You convince me that it is."

"Then tell me: what do your Toronto friends say?"

"They have turned down your proposal, Monsieur Beaumage. I am sorry. I regret it deeply. I am looking for a new and less exciting position."

"It would be wise to find one very quickly."

"I—I will get in touch with them tonight. I will tell them what has happened, to me, and ask them to change their minds. If they refuse, I shall leave immediately."

"I was hoping you would be at least that sensible. You may also tell them one more thing, Marius. Tell them that if my previous proposal is not accepted at once, there may be serious trouble at any moment."

The two guards suddenly reappeared in the room; Rosaire had touched a hidden button to summon them. "You may go now, Marius. No need for the sack on the head this time. I presume you were going to LaGarde Street when we interrupted your journey? Good, then these gentlemen will drive you there."

Scene Three

Nicole turned off the shower after one last, brief, tingling spurt of cold. She peeled the rubber shower cap from her head and her strong black hair tumbled down about her face. After a few quick rubs with the big terry towel she twisted it around her; it crossed her breasts and came high up on her long, smooth legs. Barefoot, she crossed her dressing-room and went into her bedroom.

Her bedroom—really, the master bedroom, the room she had shared with Charles. It held her vanity table, his chest of drawers; the broad double bed. But for some months now, his belongings had been in the guest room across the hall; she had slept in her double bed alone. Thus, though Charles had moved out of his own free will, she considered him evicted; she considered the room her own private preserve, and it annoyed her to find Charles here now.

He was bent over an open drawer at his chest, probing it with a long skinny arm. He wore his evening trousers, their braces still down below his waist, and a half-fastened stiff shirt. His pale hair was uncombed and stuck up on his scalp in limp tufts, like straw in winter.

Nicole had entered the room silently, and stood waiting for a minute before he noticed her. Then he looked up, started, and said, "Oh. Fresh out of collar studs across the hall."

Nicole said nothing, but still stood waiting.

"Awfully sorry to intrude," Charles said sarcastically. His speech was extremely precise, the last phase before it became thick; he was not entirely drunk, but far from sober.

He bent back to the drawer, scrabbling for his stud. He had no success, and looked up again, annoyed. He saw Nicole still standing motionless as she had been a moment before, still watching him, still waiting. He saw her long legs below the towel, and he saw a glint of her skin, dark and smooth as olive oil. She was truly a beauty, with her proud face and flowing hair. She was a woman to be desired, a woman whose pictures could have pulled millions into cinema houses, a woman to turn the head of a king. And she had been his.

Oh God, how life was full of had-beens! This woman had been his, a flourishing business had been his, a life of endless possibility had been his. And where had he gone wrong?

He drank too much. He didn't know what he wanted. He wasn't strong enough to take what he wanted when he knew it, or to hold what he wanted when he had it… Sure, accuse yourself, he thought. Accuse yourself or excuse yourself, it doesn't matter now. Beating a dead horse. This horse is dead. Pardon me, Madame Porter-Smythe, but it is of no avail, do you not see? This horse is dead. The spur is of no use…

Well, had she used the spur—in time? Yes, she tried.

He said, "Please don't let me delay you. I'll only be a minute. You want to dress, go ahead. After all, we're man and wife, aren't we? Besides, I won't peek."

Still Nicole did not move and for a minute it was impossible to guess what she was thinking. But then, without a sound, she began to cry. She cried with no sudden burying of face in hands, no shaking of her body, no dry sobs—only by drawing in her lower lip up between her teeth in vain effort to control her tears, and by the scalding water streaming down her cheeks.

Charles was shamed, penitent, angry and resentful at once. God! How had he been so entirely a fool? Nicole had loved him completely when they were married, and he had slowly made her withdraw that love. He had been afraid, from the nuptial night, of her physical ardour, her delight in passion. And then slowly, this attitude had changed; his fear of her embrace, his shyness and his dread of sex had given way to hunger for her body. But by then, of course, it was too late. He had done things to lose his case: he had fled from her into drink and nights away from home and the companions of his bachelor days, and he had let her see that he feared her, so she could feel only an increasing scorn for him—and an increasing anger at his desertion.

So they had come to this, that she cried when he invited her to dress before him. This far she had withdrawn from him.

And the anger and resentment, which were directed not entirely against himself but against her too, flooded his face with colour. Selfish little bitch, who expected him to mould his own life around her, merely because she had done him the favour of marrying him! Domineering, she was, and a nag; she'd even nagged him to cut down drinking, to spend more time with her, even once—only once—to come to bed.

She stood, beautiful, crying. His anger melted and suddenly he pitied her even more than he pitied himself. She'd had a poor shake. A husband who turned out to be no good physically and no good as a companion. A woman who could have had nearly any man, harnessed to him, getting out of the bargain only luxury, wealth, a name. If she had married him for such things, it might have served her right; but he knew as deeply as he knew anything that that was not true. True, her father had considered those things, and thought of them in making his recommendation; and Nicole was a dutiful daughter. But she had liked him, he was sure of that... before their marriage.

Why was she crying now? She could not herself have told him. Perhaps in discouragement that he was already drunk this evening; perhaps in some shame that she felt a stranger to him, that she could not bring herself to stand before him naked. Perhaps for no specific reason, but just from a general, enveloping despair of life—their life.

"Nicole!" Tears brimmed into his own eyes. He took a step toward her. She retreated.

"No, please. You must not—" She looked away from him.

He waited.

"I cannot let you touch me, take my hands, say tender things. You see? The time for that has passed. Perhaps we could be together again, forgetting everything, for this evening. But nothing would be changed. We cannot—"

"Isn't even that better than nothing? Tell me, Nicole, what are we going to do? We can't just go on like this, doing nothing. We—"

She had stopped weeping, and her voice was firmer. "We could get an annulment, you once said."

"You want that?"

"No. What would it solve?"

"It would let us part, let each go on his own way again. Perhaps we could take up our individual lives where we left them off."

"Oh, yes, easily!" she said with bitterness. "An annulment. That would have all the force of a divorce for you, or you would get yourself a divorce. And what's for me? I have my religion, my family; yes, and my conscience, my soul that I pray for. Unless you were dead I could not marry again. Unless you were dead!"

"Do you want me dead?"

"Of course not," she said sharply.

"Then this other man—you don't love him enough for that?" He barked the question, for rage had welled up again.

"What do you mean?"

"There's someone else, of course. If not, you wouldn't be thinking now that you couldn't marry again. You'd only be thinking that annulment would set you free of me. Perhaps you wouldn't want to be rid of me if there weren't someone else. Who is he?"

"You suspect my fidelity?"

"Not the fidelity of your body, my dear. But I suspect the fidelity of your love. Who do you love?"

She did not answer.

"I will refuse an annulment. Not because you could go to him if I gave you one, but because I want to hold you to me. I want you to suffer with me, to be pulled down when I am pulled down."

"What do you mean?" she asked again.

He turned his back on her and walked slowly, staggering just a little, to the door of the room. "You'll see," he said. "You'll see all too soon."

Scene Four

Ten o'clock.

The mountaintop cross blazed bright through the frosty air over Montreal. St. Catherine Street was a great glow of snarling neon and snapping mazda, bare of snow, but windswept and scoured by clouds of the ashes and sand that had been laid over the ice. People scurried along the sidewalks, men with coat-collars up and hands on their ears or holding their hats, women huddled into their fur coats. Tonight, not even a streetwalker was abroad without furs.

147

A taxi drew up in front of six-twenty LaGarde Street. Marius alighted, clung to the cab as he paid the driver, and walked with mincing, careful steps across the icy sidewalk to the entrance of the house. He pressed the bell, and when no one came immediately, tried the door; it was locked. Well, the doorman should be on the job, but at least they hadn't left the place open. He drew a key from his pocket and let himself in.

The house, which because of its heavy wooden shutters was dark from outside, was full of light. In the luxurious gaming room to his left, Francis, the senior croupier, was drawing the cover from his wheel. The other house men had readied their tables for play and were gathered at the side of the room, smoking and talking.

"Where's Barrow?" Marius asked sharply.

The house men scattered and took their positions. Francis said, "He's changing into his evening clothes."

"He should be at the door. The house should be ready to play when I arrive, Francis. As you all know," he said more loudly to the whole room. He walked angrily along the corridor to the rear door of the game-room, crossed the end of the room and went into the small office. As he was hanging up his coat he heard the door buzzer sound at the back of the hall.

He got back to the front door in time to meet Bill Gladwin, who had been admitted and relieved of his coat and hat by the doorman. Gladwin said, "Well, I guess I'm early."

"It is a little early to play, sir. I'm afraid most of our friends arrive after eleven o'clock on week nights. The bar is at your service."

"Thank you. Since no one else is here, would you join me for a drink?"

"Gladly, thank you."

They sat at a small table in the bar and were served by the boy. "Your health," Marius toasted. "We have not seen you here the last few nights, sir."

"No. And I'll tell you why. I've been hoping either my

example or my persuasion would keep Porter-Smythe away. I understand it hasn't."

"No, sir. He is here every evening, later."

"Still losing?"

"Well, sir—"

"Professional secret, eh?"

"In a sense—but you are his good friend. You will not let him know I told you. Mr. Porter-Smythe's luck has not changed, sir. It has been very, very bad and he has been more reckless just recently. Almost throwing money away."

"I thought he was at the end of his bank balance over a week ago, when you had to speak to him. Remember? He'd given you a rubber cheque."

"There has been no further trouble like that. Not until last night, that is. His cheque from two evenings ago failed to clear today, and I am worried—I don't like it, Mr. Gladwin, you must realize that. It's very bad for the house to win so consistently, and such huge amounts, from one man. There are less than a dozen men in the country, I would say, who would not be ruined by the amounts he has lost. I don't like it—and yet he would be furious if I forbade him to play here."

The front door was opened, and closed. Marius got to his feet.

"What do you suppose we can do with him?" Gladwin wondered.

Marius said graciously, "If you have any suggestions—" and left the sentence unfinished as he bowed slightly and moved away.

Gladwin sat staring at his drink. Someone entered the room, but he did not look up until a voice called, "Hello, gloomy!"

Linda had come into the room with Charles Porter-Smythe. Bill got to his feet and said, "Hi, you two. What brings you here?"

"The free liquor," Linda said immediately.

"Just what you'd expect," Charles said simultaneously.

"And why are we here together?" Linda asked. "Go on, you're dying to know, you old gossip."

"I can guess."

"I'll tell you. In all gory detail. Charles had a fight with Nicole and she wouldn't come out with him. He went to drink it off at the Chatham and I was there with the dullest character in Montreal, who didn't believe in gambling and wouldn't come here. So naturally I left him there to cool his heels and made Charles bring me here."

"Naturally," agreed Gladwin.

"I was coming anyway," Charles said mildly.

"To gamble with what?" Bill asked unpleasantly.

"Wha' you mean, with what?"

"Surely you know you're out of cash again. How much have you gambled away now?"

"How d'you know I'm out o' cash?"

"Your cheques are elastic again."

"Pardon me. I've got to go give Marius hell."

"Oh, I made him tell me. Give me hell for not minding my own business."

"Consider it done."

Linda said, "Are you two just going to stand here and fight? Because if so, I'll go get myself a drink."

Gladwin and Charles continued to glare at one another and Linda gave a little laugh, left them and went to sit on a bar stool.

Gladwin said, "I've told you before you're being an inconceivably stupid ass, so I suppose it won't do me any good to repeat myself."

Charles gave him a crooked leer. "Maybe I want to be ruined. Ever think of that?"

"What's wrong?"

"I don't like myself anymore. An' the only way I can figure out to make me like myself again is break the bank in this damned place. Take it for about five hundred thousand."

"Just how much have you lost trying to do this?"

"Just about a hundred thousand, I guess. No, I don't know—maybe a hundred and fifty, if I'm drawing rubber cheques again. Not a loss, though, William, my boy. Investment. Returns start to come in when my luck changes."

"Oh, don't be so God-damned stupid!"

Charles turned sharply, wavered, caught his balance and went out.

Linda called to Bill, "That's no way to handle him."

"And you would know how to do it?"

"I know. Let's get Nicole to have him committed as an alcoholic."

"Just full of bright ideas, aren't you!"

"You're in a sweet bloody mood tonight," Linda said pleasantly, and followed Charles out of the room.

Franz, urbane in his evening clothes, tall and very straight, came into the bar a moment after she had left. His fair skin was still flushed from the cold outside and he chafed his hands slowly, one over the other. His eyes were narrowed, his expression one of annoyance.

"Good evening, Bill. Boy, a brandy."

"Hello, Franz."

"I am glad to find you here alone. We have a little business to transact."

"Oh—my investment?"

"Yes." Franz sat down, brought out a chequebook and pen, and wrote.

"Another five thousand?"

"Ten. Our venture is successful."

"Our venture is a mint. What is it? Can't you tell me?"

"Please do be content to accept another golden egg."

"How much of this does Marius get?"

Franz started. "What? What do you mean?"

Gladwin laughed. "I mean, how much of your share? He gets a bit of mine."

"Oh—I am lucky in this house. I do not lose."

"I knew you two were in cahoots, from the night you

brought us here. Marius picked a good man to fill his house."

"Ah, yes," Franz laughed casually. "I am an expert shill."

"I'll say. Marius leaves you, but before he goes he presents his card with a flourish. 'Bring your friends here, Mr. Loebek, and you will never lose. Six-twenty LaGarde…'"

Six-twenty LaGarde. Of course. Six-twenty LaGarde. There was a sudden meshing of memories in Gladwin's mind, and he stared blankly away from Franz for a minute, recalling something.

"What's wrong?"

"This was Morrie Winter's house!"

"Was it?"

"Of course. You telephoned me, remember, and got me to call Beaumage. The house was to be closed."

"Oh. Yes."

"Jesus!"

"What is it?"

"I'm ten percent responsible for the ruination of Charles."

"Charles is responsible for his own ruin," Franz said flatly.

"No, dammit, we are. Good God, I was a fool to go into this thing blind! Why'd I make the mistake of trusting you?"

"Aren't you being a bit—Oh, there she is again!" Franz said with great annoyance. "Watch her start another scene."

Gladwin glanced over his shoulder and saw Linda at the doorway. She was looking at Franz. "Oh. You're still here," she said coldly. "Boy, bring me a Scotch and water to the gaming room." She turned away from them.

She had met Franz just when she was coming into the house. He had said pleasantly enough, "Good evening, Linda." She had slapped him.

Perhaps that way would work. Perhaps she could make him angry enough to take her again. And if he took her once, twice more—no, once more; she would make once be enough—then he would not be able to let her go. He would be caught.

But even as she thought this she doubted her power over him, her ability to draw him back. And she raged within herself. She stood with her back to him and longed to turn and look at him again, to go up to him and—either make love to him or kill him.

The door was just opening now, and she watched absently. The house was filling with people and all the games were in swing—with Charles, as usual, at the crap table. Marius had glanced toward the door and saw Rosaire entering, accompanied by a broad and black-haired man who carried a capacious briefcase.

Marius hurried serviley toward them, and Rosaire said clearly, with a kindly smile to Marius, "Good evening. You see, I have brought my associate, Jean-Paul the collector."

"Of course, Monsieur Beaumage. Shall we talk later?"

"Yes, later."

Marius bowed himself away. Minutes later, he went back to glance in the hallway; Jean-Paul was still there, idling near the doorway of the gaming room. Jean-Paul made him nervous.

What was going on? Had Rosaire really brought him to carry home his cut of the night's take? Franz would never permit it, and then— He wanted to talk to Franz, but the fool had been arguing with Gladwin ever since he arrived.

What would Franz do? He would stay, of course, until the play was over. He would realize eventually that Rosaire was in the house, and would find out why. Then would he reveal himself to Rosaire? Marius wished fervently that he could slip away and leave them to argue it out. That was impossible—unless he wanted to leave and never return. Perhaps he would take that course. Wait and see. If life was in danger...

He went back into the game-room. Someone was calling him—Rosaire.

He came back to the crap table and said, "Yes, Monsieur Beaumage?"

"Marius, have you any word for me?"

"I'm sorry, sir. Not yet."

"I trust there will be news before I leave."

Scene Five

"We have been completely through this thing four times now," Franz said wearily, "with varying degrees of recrimination. I see no point in discussing it further."

"I'm not going to stop until I convince you you've done us all a lot of harm," Gladwin replied.

They sat in a little private office behind the gaming room. The air was heavy and blue with cigarette smoke. They had been sitting there for hours.

"Listen to me, my friend. You, above all, should not complain of my actions. Recall our first talk in Montreal? You wanted me to represent myself as a man of wealth, a moneyed aristocrat. Under such false pretenses I would become a friend of your friends, I would become a desirable person to employ, and one of them would offer me a position."

"And you'd have given them good value for your salary, I felt sure. No, there was nothing wrong with that, Franz. It was just a question of putting on front. It wasn't any more dishonest than getting a bank loan to start off a new business—borrowing money you didn't have, but knew you could get later, to create an immediate impression. But you took my success formula and perverted it into something to bilk my friends."

"No one has been bilked," Franz said sharply. "This is a square house."

"Perhaps. But a lamb's been slaughtered."

"I did not wish that."

"You weren't able to control the evil aspects of the

business, once you started it. And perhaps you wanted Charles ruined."

"What do you mean by that?"

"You're in love with Nicole, aren't you? And she's in love with you, but won't leave Charles. But she might leave a ruined Charles."

"Maybe you think I would hire a gang of thugs, to have him killed."

"Maybe you haven't faced up to your own thoughts on this. Search them. It would be easier to win Nicole with Charles disgraced, wouldn't it? You've thought that, haven't you?"

There was a distinct but muffled *pop*, originating somewhere in the neighborhood, which jarred the building just perceptibly.

"I—What do you suppose that was?"

Gladwin shrugged. "Sewer gas explosion."

"Come! At this time of year?"

"Well, some idiot probably just blew up a gas stove, then."

The door opened, showing the outer rooms in darkness. Marius entered and said, "Everyone has gone. I have locked up."

"Did you hear that explosion?"

"I heard something. It seemed to come from below, perhaps from the cellar of the house next door."

Franz frowned. "Rosaire was here tonight. Perhaps I am too apprehensive—Listen."

They were completely silent for as long as one can hold his breath. No sound came to them.

"All right, close the door," Franz said briskly. "You have tonight's proceeds? Good, we proceed to break up a partnership."

Gladwin drew out his wallet and took from it the ten thousand dollar cheque Franz had given him some hours earlier. He held the cheque in front of him, gazed at it for a moment, and then deliberately tore it into bits. "I've already taken my money back," he said. "I don't want a profit on this deal. You certainly don't have to divide tonight's take with me. The partnership is dissolved. I withdraw."

Franz said angrily, "As you wish. What charity do you wish to receive your share?"

"Charles."

"No."

"Then you can fling it in the St. Lawrence, or keep it yourself."

"Thank you." Franz paused. Then he said, "Marius will take you to the door."

"Not yet," Gladwin said calmly.

"Have we further business?"

"I'm not dissolving the partnership. I'm dissolving the enterprise."

"Oh? Why—and how?"

"It's obvious why. I hate seeing my friends ruined. How? With your consent, I hope. Surely you've made enough money from it! Get out of the business, for everyone's sake, and for your own. Your secret can't possibly be kept much longer, and when it's out you're through in Montreal."

"I cannot stop. You are entirely wrong if you think I entered this business to make money, to ruin Charles, to gain power. I became a gambler for one reason: to destroy Rosaire Beaumage."

Marius, who had remained silent until now, entered the conversation: "It is true. Franz has refused any compromise with Beaumage. This matter is reaching a head."

"You're a fool to buck Beaumage."

"Not buck him. Fight him."

"And suppose you win? Then what? You'd take his place. You wouldn't be able to get out of it. Anyway, by then there'd be nothing you could do in this city. Know something? I think I'd as soon have Beaumage running gambling, as have you."

"You have become very bitter about me, suddenly."

"I feel I've been made a fool, deceived. It makes a man resentful."

"You do not know Beaumage, the evil murderer, or you would not say I am not better."

"I don't have to know Beaumage. I know you. Maybe I'll regret this tomorrow, Franz. But tonight I think you're a greedy, arrogant fool." Gladwin stood and strode to the door. He turned the knob.

Before he could fling open the door it was torn from his grasp and swung violently wide. A rush of unbearably hot air, bearing with it dark, oily smoke, burst into the room. Gladwin, full in the path of this blast, staggered back coughing, his hands on his burning eyes. Franz and Marius started to their feet.

"Fire. Started with that little explosion we heard," Franz said rapidly.

"Rosaire! His man Jean-Paul was with him tonight."

"Made terrific headway," Franz gasped. He drew his handkerchief and covered his nose and mouth. He went to the doorway and peered through the dense, torrid smoke.

At the far end of the gaming room, tongues of orange flame leaped from the corridor, short, then long, the long ones reaching nearly to the far side of the room.

They lit up the smoke in a variable, cloudy pattern like floodlights playing on fog. The roar of the flames was heavy and deep-throated, steady as the blast of a giant blow-torch, complemented by a crackling from tinder-dry wood.

The office was filled with smoke now and the dim glow reaching in from the open door was no help to vision. They closed their smarting eyes and groped.

"Front door is cut off," Franz choked.

"Windows here," Gladwin yelled, and knocked over a chair as he careened to the rear of the room.

"Barred."

"Washroom, here. Wet handkerchiefs over our faces. Make it to a top floor and get out onto a roof."

"Never make it!" Gladwin mouthed. "Smoke and heat worse upstairs. Try the front door."

"Impossible!"

They were all in the washroom now. Franz turned the faucet; it spurted boiling water, then hissed steam. He shut it off. Ripping the lid off the toilet tank he plunged his hand inside, soaking the handkerchief. The coolness of the water was a blessing to his eyes, the wet cloth pressed against his face let him breathe. The others followed his example.

There was a heavy, jarring crash from the front of the house, with a rending, splintering sound. For a minute the flames crackled wildly; then the roar seemed louder than before.

"What—?"

"Cellar stairway," Marius guessed. "Come on."

They groped together from the washroom to the office, out into the furnace heat of the gaming room and then through its rear door into the back of the corridor. At the front of the house, the corridor was a mass of flame, bright yellow now.

"Stairs—right here!" Franz shouted.

"I'm for the front door." Gladwin dashed past them, down the corridor and into the inferno.

They did not stop to watch him. They reached the bottom of the stairs and ran upward, around the landing, up to the second floor. The heat seared their skin.

Franz kicked at the window at the top of the stairs. His heel cracked into the frame, and the window burst outward. Smoke and heat tore past them as they bent out to gasp clean air.

"Out—here?" Marius asked.

"No. Straight drop down. Come, up again."

The smoky air was so thick as they went along the second-floor corridor that it gave Franz the impression of wading through deep water. Every step was as full of effort as steps against a rip-tide. The lungs cried for air and there was no air, only heat and the choking smoke.

They reached the stairs to the third floor. They stumbled as they started up these stairs and Marius began crawling upwards on his hands and knees. The heat seemed to come in waves now, as though the fire were a ravening beast, gulping at the house, then drawing back to suck in its food, and gulping again. The orange haze of the smoke was bright as the mist before a rising sun, and the sounds of the fire's destruction were awesome—the roar, the crackle; the hiss, the crash of severed beams.

Franz reached the top of the stairs and opened the first door to his right. Marius flung himself past the door and when it was closed they were in a room the smoke and heat had not yet fully penetrated. The room was hot, but its heat seemed like that of a tropic day rather than that of a furnace.

They ran to the room's window. The house, built a storey higher than the next on the street, had side windows here on the third floor which overlooked the adjacent roof. This had formed the basis for Franz' plan of escape.

But there was no escape from this window. Below it sloped a sharply-angled, snow-covered, treacherous roof. The pitch of this roof would make it impossible to get a foothold.

"Other side of the house!" Franz panted. "Maybe a flat roof over there."

In an instant they were back at the door of the room; as they turned its knob, it virtually exploded into the room. One look showed them the flames had now reached the third floor. The corridor was impossible.

Their combined weight wrestled the door shut. Franz ran back to the window and flung it wide. He looked again at the steeply-sloped roof outside the window; then he climbed out onto the sill.

"You cannot make it!" Marius screamed.

"We cannot go back."

The ridge of the roof was above Franz as he stood on

the window sill. He crouched and jumped powerfully up-ward.

He landed flat on the slope, his fingers across the ridge. Then slowly, inexorably, the snow surface beneath them began to shift and he slipped by inches down the roof. His fingers clawed for the ridge, and found only snow that gave beneath his grasp.

His downward slide became more rapid; the move-ment of snow off the roof was cumulative, and was turn-ing into a small avalanche.

He clawed with fingers, dug with toes, tried to brace with elbows and knees; nothing slowed him. Then Marius, reaching far out of the window, grabbed a handful of cloth at the back of his jacket and held him. Marius pulled him toward the window, and there he could catch the rough stones in a wall of his house, and hold.

That was the method for climbing! In a minute the snow slide had stopped. Calling to Marius to release him, Franz began to inch his way up the steep roof, pressing his body into the angle between the roof and the wall of this house, clinging to the stone with his fingers. In less than a minute he was astride the ridge. And Marius, seeing how he had done this, followed him to the peak.

They were safe.

They crossed the roof, swinging along with one foot on either side of the peak, and then saw, some feet below them, the flat roof of the next house. It was an easy jump to reach it.

Below, in the street, it was light as day with the flames from the blazing house. Sirens howled. Fire engines had already arrived on the scene, and more were coming.

Directly opposite the house where they now stood, a long black ambulance drew up. The two attendants, dark heavy coats incongruous over their white uniforms, brought the stretcher from their vehicle and stood beside it, ready, waiting.

Scene Six

It was daylight when Rosaire reached his own suite in the house in Outrement. Then for a while he stayed in his office, poring over accounts.

It was too early yet to tell how the evening had gone, but they had done their work thoroughly. One of his men had reported on the fire—a spectacular fire. Jean-Paul, with his gallon of gasoline to pour over the junk piled in the basement of the LaGarde Street house, and his fuse that set the fire going after they had left, was an efficient worker.

He yawned. He would sleep well.

He shut off the lights in his office and went into his bedroom. As always, he checked the room. His eyes swept over it and found nothing out of place. Then he went to the window and raised it to provide fresh air for his sleep.

He stepped back from the window... and halted suddenly. The window was always kept locked. This time, it had not been locked. Panicky, he stepped to the window again and examined it again.

The lock was broken.

He spun about in terror as though avoiding a blow, turning to face an opponent who had crept up behind him. He scanned the room.

Nothing was out of place, no one was in sight.

He scurried to the small lamp table beside his bed and yanked open its drawer. He pawed for his gun. His gun was not in the drawer.

His bathroom door slowly opened.

Franz said, "It is here, Beaumage. I have it." The revolver was level in his hand, pointed at Rosaire's heart.

"*Mon dieu!*" Rosaire breathed. His face was a mask of terror, the lips pulled hysterically down at their corners, the eyes staring wide.

"I do not believe we have met."

"I—I know who you are."

"Good. Then you know why I have come."

"No," Rosaire said with a flash of bravado. "Surely you're not so foolish as to come here to threaten me?"

"Of what use are threats? I have come here to kill you. I should tell you why. Because you killed Morrie Winter and Willie Cameron. Because tonight you killed Bill Gladwin."

"It is a lie." Rosaire retreated slowly to his bedside table.

"Ah. Perhaps you have a call-button beneath that table? Press it, by all means. You'll be dead before help can come."

"You would shoot me in cold blood?"

"You ask me that? You, who murder in cold blood?"

"Have you thought that you will die, if you kill me? Have you thought how you may die? My men are very loyal."

"Your face is very white, Beaumage. I did not think to find you such a coward."

"Who is not frightened of a madman?"

"Or of a mad dog? I do this city, this country, a greater service than I ever have done it before."

Four things happened, in such close sequence that they seem simultaneous. The door of Rosaire's bedroom first opened; Rosaire threw himself to the floor; Franz fired; Jean-Paul, hurtling through the door, flung his automatic pistol with deadly accuracy at Franz' arm and knocked spinning the gun he had held.

Jean-Paul, carried on by the momentum of his rush, overwhelmed Franz and flattened him on the floor. Behind him two more of Rosaire's men came more carefully into the room, levelling their revolvers. An instant later the taxi driver, Jules Trebonne, was prodded through the door by the pistol of yet another man. His hands were tied behind his back.

Rosaire picked himself slowly up from the floor.

One of the men collected the two guns which had clattered into a corner of the room. When he saw the gun safe, Jean-Paul clambered to his feet and allowed Franz to rise.

"Jean-Paul," Rosaire said, "our protective measures must be revised."

"It is true," the big man puffed. "It was a mistake, to put on the patrol only when you are in the house. We must always have the patrol. Luckily, when the men began their rounds they found this cow of a taxi-driver skulking at the rear of the house. And I was suspicious, and it is lucky I was suspicious soon enough."

"Monsieur Loebek," Rosaire said politely, "are there any more statements you wish to make to me?"

Franz laughed. "What is the point? It seems I've lost another round. The last round, of course. How do you propose to kill me, Beaumage? Quickly, or slowly?"

"Thus the hero speaks. No doubt it is immaterial to you? If there is torture, you will not flinch. If death comes slowly, you will still spit in my face at the end as I watch you die. Ah, Loebek, how I admire you men of great physical courage! You are so vastly superior to me, the little rabbit Rosaire, who cringes at the slightest danger, who is but a jelly of nerves! It is a great gift, this physical courage."

"Come, this is not a time for oratory. Do what you intend. But let Jules go—"

"Hah, the hero again! 'Do what you want with me, but let my follower go free. He did not know what he was doing. It was my responsibility and I am willing to take the consequences.'"

"—or do not let him go, as you wish. He knew he was taking a risk. He only did not know how great was the risk."

Jules muttered something in French, which could only have been heard by Jean-Paul. "More of that and you will have bloody ears," Jean-Paul told him grimly.

Rosaire had seated himself on his bed, lighted a cigarette, and relaxed. He sat watching Franz with a small smile on his face, a smile not of triumph nor of relief nor yet even of disdain, but of something like condescension. And Franz, who did not fear to meet his gaze, looked at him, and easily about the room, and back to him again. Franz stood loosely, his arms hanging at his sides, his weight distributed on spread legs—disarmed and menaced by armed men and in a sense helpless, but ready to resist any new move.

Rosaire said, "I will disappoint you. I will not kill you."

He waited. Franz made no change in his posture, but stared at him. He said, "I had hoped to kill you this evening. It meant a great deal of trouble. Now I see I have troubled myself needlessly."

"Go on," Franz invited.

"You are such a fool, Loebek, that I shall leave you to kill yourself. It is not merely that I do not fear you any longer; I wish to see how you will entangle yourself next, how you arrange your fate. Go."

Jean-Paul stirred uneasily.

"No, Jean-Paul. Of course I mean this. Let them go."

"Untie the cab driver," Jean-Paul grumbled.

"I expect you to make another attempt on my life. But that is easily guarded against. I intend to be most carefully guarded until you have run your course, Loebek. But it will not be long."

"You are very sure of yourself, Beaumage."

"No, no, my friend. Of you."

Franz and Jules Trebonne were guided out through Rosaire's office, out the front door of the house. They walked away down the drive and along the street a block to where the cab was parked.

"If you had stayed in your cab and waited, as I said," Franz groaned. "If you had done as I told you—well, it might have come out differently."

"I was worried about you. I went to see if—"

"Well, it does not matter. It does not matter now."

SEVEN

Scene One

"It looks as though he may have died in the fire," the voice on the telephone said.

C.C. Warren was very annoyed at the voice. "Garfield, that's an uncommonly indefinite statement for you to make," he complained.

"I can't locate him at—"

"I don't care where you *can't* locate him. Are you prepared to say definitely he died in the fire?"

"No, I—"

"Well then, keep looking. I have a very vital reason for wanting to see him. Either establish that he was caught in that fire, or find him for me."

Warren hung up and turned his attention again to the pile of morning letters stacked neatly before him. He had read through six lengthy missives, on subjects ranging from the quality of iron ore found on one of his Northern Labrador properties to the state of the Canadian market for frozen peas, when his buzzer sounded.

"Warren," he responded, into the telephone.

"It's Garfield. Well, sir, believe me, this was a really hard one to track—"

"Garfield, don't waste my time with editorial comment. Did you find Porter-Smythe?"

"Yes, sir."

"Good."

"The police didn't know whether he'd been burnt up. His household said he hadn't been since yesterday. He wasn't at his office, either."

"Well, where was he?"

"After the fire he'd gone to the apartment of a friend of his, Barney Carr, and spent the night there. It was interesting how I tracked that—"

"Not to me, Garfield. I expect you to get results but I'm not interested in hearing about your brilliant detective work in detail. Did you speak to Porter-Smythe himself?"

"Yes. He's not in very good shape. I told him I was calling for you, and you wanted to see him most urgently. He said he'd come see you this afternoon."

"I told you I wanted to see him this morning!" Warren snapped.

"I told him that, too. He said he'd be around."

"When?"

"As soon as he could. I expect that would be after a long, cold shower, some black coffee, a sedative and a little intravenous glucose."

"All right, send your bill," Warren said abruptly, and hung up.

Warren devoted himself to the problem of whether he should sell one of his gold mines. The Syndicate had made an excellent offer. It took Warren ten minutes to decide to sell, and more than an hour, at his desk and on the telephone, arranging the paperwork necessary to complete the sale.

At the end of this time his blonde secretary came into the office with letters for his signature and said, "Mr. Porter-Smythe is waiting to see you."

"Send him in."

Warren well remembered old Porter-Smythe, Charles' father; gigantic, with a leontine mane of grey hair, a roaring imperious voice. The son resembled the father uncannily, like a line drawing done with a pantograph; each line the same, and yet the whole in smaller scale. Charles was a lion cub who had never grown to be a lion, who had stayed small and puny until his form and features began to age slightly, to sharpen. If his father been a lion, he was a—jackal? No, no, he hadn't the character of a jackal. Nor of a hyena. A large, lion-clipped French poodle, Warren thought suddenly; an aging poodle.

Warren concealed perfectly his contemptuous thoughts, and got up to greet Charles warmly. He came from behind his desk and pumped warmly at Charles' flaccid hand. "It's good—it's a relief to see you. We were afraid you'd been caught in that fire, you know."

"Fire?" Charles asked vaguely.

"At the gambling house. It burnt to a shell last night."

"Good heavens! Must have been after I left. How did it happen?"

"No one seems to know. Young Gladwin died in the fire—Oh, I'm sorry. He was one of your friends, I know, and you wouldn't have heard. I didn't mean to break the news to you in that way."

"Bill Gladwin—burnt up in a fire?"

"He was caught in the building."

"Oh." Charles' voice was wooden, and his reaction of a straw man. He suddenly and awkwardly sat in a chair, the force of his collapse leaving him almost without breath. He put his head far back and inhaled deeply through his open mouth. After a minute Warren came to him solicitously with a big silver box of cigarettes. Charles took one, and lighting it, smoked tremblingly.

Warren said, "Please just relax. I am very busy this morning, but I can delay other matters. I am afraid we must have a serious discussion, and I do not want to begin while you're so upset."

Charles asked, "What must we discuss?" His voice was dull.

"Please don't think of it for a moment. Pardon me, I'll get the rest of these documents off my desk."

Charles oozed clammy, cold perspiration and thought of fire, and Bill Gladwin, and himself, and being drunken, and how he might have died. His thoughts started out in shock and sorrow for Gladwin and ended neurotically in horror and disgust and fear of himself. The gambling house had burned. Gladwin had burned; it might well have been he. Charles shuddered, vividly seeing flames.

Warren had cleared everything from his desk. He stared for a time with his bug-like eyes at Charles, but Charles was sunk in himself. Warren cleared his throat and said brusquely, "I wish this could wait, Charles, but I'm afraid it can't."

"Oh. Oh, yes. What?"

"I hold your personal note for one hundred thousand dollars."

Charles stood, very slowly. He held himself stiffly. His voice was icy: "I beg your pardon?"

"I have your note for one hundred thousand dollars. A perfectly legal document, witnessed and signed. Payable on demand. And of course, it is has been endorsed over to me and is in my possession legally. I bought it from your friend Winslow."

"I see."

Charles stared at Warren. The great, unblinking, nightmare eyes behind the glasses met his gaze without wavering. Charles was outraged and disgusted. He had gone to Winslow when he might have gone to a bank. And Winslow had betrayed him.

"You—have my note?" he asked again slowly, thinking of the details of the only thing he could do.

"Yes."

"It is a demand note. And I am to understand you demand payment?"

"In a—manner of speaking. I don't want to be unreasonable, Charles. I'm prepared—"

"To discuss the details of taking over my business. Of course. You wanted my business, Warren. Now you've got the weapon that will give it to you."

"You hardly do me justice, Charles. I—"

"Presuming that you demand payment of the note, I naturally have three legal days of grace in which to meet it. Well, sorry to disappoint you, Warren, but you won't get Porter Bolt and Screw. I'll sell it for what I can get, to pay the note. And I can find a buyer. There are other men in the country with money—and with such unshakable positions they will be glad to deal with me, even when I explain that will displease you."

"Now, Charles, be fair. You don't think very highly of me—because I'm a good, hard businessman and you're not. I didn't get where I am today without being ruthless, but my ruthlessness means, in the long run, successful businesses and steady income for my employees; good dividends for my associates and my stockholders. You see only the bad side."

"I see that you want to expropriate my business."

"Let's go back a step. God knows what Winslow might have done with that note—who he might have sold you out to. When I was informed, this morning, that the note was for sale, I took quick steps to obtain it. I may add that I had to pay considerably more than its face value. I think I did you a favour."

"And now you want to do me another favor; you want to run my business for me. Oh, I can see I've been foolish. I owe you a considerable debt for what you've done. But I don't owe you my business."

"Shall I give it back so you can sign another one, some evening when you're drinking and gambling?"

"It's clear I can't gamble anymore. The gambling house is gone, and I won't be searching for a new one. I shall be far more careful now, I assure you."

"Charles, you stated your only alternatives. You can sell the business to someone else to pay me—since, naturally, I must be paid—or you can keep an interest in the business and let me take over its management. Wouldn't the latter be a better solution? You have a wonderful small business, Charles, a business your father built as solid as a rock. And you've been letting it fall apart. You must face the fact that you aren't a businessman. It's no disgrace, God knows; your other talents may outweigh business aptitude. But you've been merely controlling this firm, not managing it. It needs a strong hand. I'll give it that, and I'll turn it into an income-producer that will bring you more for your shares than you now get from the entire ownership. Consider that. And consider the load it would lift from you: no more striving to deal with dull routine, no more trying to take your father's place. You aren't suited for that and you've hated it, I know you have. I'll take that load, gladly."

"And the business."

"And the business. Would you rather someone else had it? Would you rather, for instance, Franz Loebek had it?"

"What makes you ask that rather silly question?"

"I see I must tell you about Franz, as well. You said just now you weren't likely to gamble again; you weren't likely to seek out another gambling house. But what if Franz opens another house and takes you to it?"

"You mean, I suppose, that Franz ran that house."

"You needn't take my word for it. A number of others know. Franz—I suppose you considered him your friend—has not done too well in your interests, has he? Until last night you were so deeply in debt to him that your business might have gone to him. And he's taking advantage of your friendship to seduce your wife —"

"Stop, Warren!" Charles shouted.

"I'm sorry. To fall in love with Nicole, then."

"That's a particularly foul lie, Warren. You were being most convincing, I admit. But you've gone much too far. If Nicole and I have not been close, it's been my fault—not the work of a third person. As for its being Franz—"

"Ask her. Or ask him. I don't care. But remember all I've said. You must decide, and you must settle. You—"

Charles had left the office without speaking to him again.

As he went away thoughts of Franz and Nicole conflicted in his mind with thought of the other problem: No matter what I do, his mind repeated again and again, I've lost the business.

Scene Two

After the door bell had rung, and rung, and rung, the man outside began to beat on the door. Franz had been determined not to answer, but the man was so persistent—and after all that had happened, it was impossible to guess who it might be, how important might be the message.

He went very quietly to the apartment door and in an interval between the pounding blows said, "Yes? What is it?"

"It's Burns. That you, Squadron-Leader?"

"What do you want?"

"I want some angles for a story. And may write a worse story if I don't talk to you, than if I do."

"Blackmail is a weapon fools use on cowards, Burns."

"I'm only using it for shock value. I want to get that door open so I can talk to you."

"About what? Start again."

"Sure. I'll quote: 'The time has come, the walrus said—'"

Franz opened the door. "To talk of what specific things?"

"What's going to happen," Burns said brightly. He came in, swept off his fedora and deposited a small drift of snow on the floor of the entry; snapped open his floppy coat and filled the air for an instant with powdered snow-crystals. "Wonderful morning, Squadron-Leader. Snow coming quietly down in tiny flakes from a bright sky. Crunching, snapping cold. Thanks for your fire. It cost me my whole night's sleep, but it stopped me drinking soon enough to enjoy this morning."

"Thank Rosaire for the fire."

"Did you find him last night, after I told you his address?"

"Nothing happened. Therefore it is of no consequence to whether or not I found him."

"It might be, it might be. You remember I came in asking what was going to happen; want me to be more specific?"

"I'm sure you will be."

"I wonder what the next step in the great struggle will be. You see, I like to think I ride herd on this town pretty closely. It isn't entirely a profession, with me. This town's my hobby, in a way. I love it and I keep wondering what's going to happen to it. Rosaire happened to it, and that wasn't good—it was about the worst thing since the Iroquois massacred the early settlers. Then you came into the picture and the big fight started. You were out to get Rosaire's scalp, weren't you? But it hasn't been going very well."

"No." Franz said wearily. "It has not gone well."

"I can see the way it built up. First, Rosaire killed Morrie Winter—"

"What?"

"You suspected that, didn't you?"

"Of course. Pardon me. I'm so surprised only because I thought no one else suspected."

"I got a few basic rumors and it was just a matter of simple addition. Then—"

"He killed Willie Cameron."

"Oh. I forgot about that. It adds in, all right. But after that you had your innings. Things went pretty smoothly, until last night. Score for last night: Gladwin dead, and your house gone. Now what do you plan to do about Rosaire?"

"Kill him."

"Bravo! How?"

"I—I have not planned that."

"Rosaire knows you're gunning for him, of course. Is he gunning for you?"

"No," Franz said shortly. "He is waiting for me to commit suicide."

Scene Three

The blonde secretary looked up, startled, from typing. She said rapidly, clearly, "Miss Warren, I'm afraid your father—" She stopped as the slamming of the door to C.C. Warren's private office cut off the rest of her sentence.

Warren glared as his door opened and closed. Two men were sitting in his office opposite his desk. "Linda," he said. "Wasn't Miss Johnson at her desk? I told her no one was to come in. I'm sorry, I'll have to ask—"

"I'll wait," Linda said tightly. She threw herself into a chair at the side of the office.

Warren coloured. He stood. "Mr. Cartwright, Mr. Smith." The two men rose. "Gentlemen, my daughter." They bowed. Linda nodded her head.

Warren did not resume his seat. "Well, I think that about settles the thing," he said smoothly. "I will prepare the papers and have them ready for delivery tomorrow at two o'clock. You will bring the certified cheque when you come, of course. If there are any minor details our counsel can meet to settle them."

He ushered the men from his office and came back angrily to face Linda. "What's wrong with you? Do you think this office is a place where I play games? It's possible you may have cost me two hundred thousand dollars in the sale of that mine."

"Take it off my allowance."

"Is there some major crisis in your life? What do you want?"

"Information, and I've got tired combing the city for it. Nobody knows anything about the fire last night. The

173

morning *Clarion* said Bill Gladwin had been killed—and nothing more. Their editor won't even guess if anyone else was killed. None of the other papers know anything. The police won't tell me anything, and the fire department has no information. What do you know?"

"What is so vital about all this?"

"I've got very good reason to think some friends of mine were there in the place last night, when it burned, and didn't get out. I've been all over town trying to find out."

"Well—you might have phoned me."

"I was too tired of stalls. I came."

"Who are you worried about?"

She breathed deeply of cigarette smoke, took the cigarette away from her face, and leaned toward him. In her voice was tension she could not hide. "What happened to Franz?"

"Loebek? I don't know."

"Early this morning I went to his apartment," she said, her eyes vacant and staring as though she was talking to herself. "No one was there. Then I've phoned, and phoned. He doesn't answer his phone. I don't know what to do. I don't—"

"I thought you were through with Loebek."

"I guess I only wanted to be." She got up slowly and went limply toward the door of the office, without a trace of the proud walk that was almost her trademark.

"Charles Porter-Smythe is all right," Warren told her.

She turned. She tossed her great mane of smooth hair back and lifted her chin as she looked at him again, but her eyes still were dull and her voice very quiet. "Oh? Good. I'm glad, I am glad."

"Charles was here in the office just an hour ago. We had a business discussion. It seems as though I'll have to manage his business for him, to keep it out of the hands of gamblers."

"What do you mean?"

"I don't want to talk about it. Especially not today."

"Then you shouldn't have started to talk about it. Come," she said angrily and commandingly, "what do you mean?"

"I bought his note."

"That was rather despicable of you, wasn't it?"

"Linda, I don't expect you to understand me. Once in a while, though, you might try and give me credit for motives a little higher than those of a cheap loan-shark."

"Charles is a person I like. You can't expect me to be wildly enthusiastic when you're ruining him."

"Wait a minute. Your precious Franz Loebek tried to ruin him. I'm saving him."

"I'm a little upset today, and perhaps I shouldn't go on," Linda said harshly. "But it seems as good a time as any to tell you what I really hate about you, Father. You're incapable of seeing yourself the way you really are. You think you're a little tin god, benefactor of the human race, and of each individual you reach out to touch. Kneel, kiss the ring, and I bestow on you the benediction of capitalism. I am prince of capitalism and wherever my eye falls, the wilderness vomits up its riches. I make men slaves to their greater happiness and the greater glory of capitalism. I turn the wheels—"

"I didn't know you'd been going to Communist meetings," Warren said bitingly.

"I don't like Communists either. I don't like people who want to tie strings around other people and dance them around. And those who claim they're doing it for the good of the puppets are the worst kind. Oh, I haven't any political or social consciousness, Father. You know that perfectly well. I'll take any kind of system that leaves people reasonably alone. But running people—"

"You run anybody you can run. You're talking out of character. You've spent your whole life pushing people into doing things for you—and you know it."

"Leave my personal life out of this. We're talking on

a bigger scale. Certainly I push people around —for my good, and I let them know it. I don't tell them what a great favour I'm doing them. You relax, Colonel. Don't let me ever hear you say how you saved Charles, not ever again."

"What are you trying to get out of all this?" Warren's voice was angry, his macroscopic eyes more glaring.

"Nothing but self-satisfaction."

"It may be very dearly bought, young woman."

Linda stood proudly, hands at her sides, head back. She smiled. She said, "Go on."

"I'm tired of your airs, your criticism, your lack of appreciation. I brought you up from a little slum gamin into what you are now, and I want some recognition for that. You haven't been easy to train, but I've trained you. I've made you a fine, desirable specimen of woman. I want you to realize that—that I've given you your will, your sense of values—"

"You've made me nothing. I'd be a desirable woman anywhere, and I know it. I had my will before you found me, and I've still got it. You haven't broken it—maybe you haven't tried—but you haven't moulded it either. I grew up the way I wanted. I got the things I wanted for myself, and I always will."

"All I want from you is the respect of one strong person for another."

"You—strong?"

"Strong enough to throw you away and break you."

"Perhaps you think I'm not strong enough to walk away from you and take care of myself. Perhaps you think I won't leave you, and all the things you've given me, sometime. Is that so? Push me. Go on, push me once more."

"I want you to change. Remember that. I want to see the change. You've gone too far; you must back-track—"

"That was the push." She stripped off her beaver coat and flung it at him; it landed crumpled at his feet. "It's too cold to walk out in underwear," she said, "or you could have the dress. You'll have it soon enough. And I won't be going back to the house, so you can have fun selling my other clothes."

Warren gasped. "You little fool!"

"Here!" she threw her handbag back to him. "My bank book is in there. But don't begin to think I'm without resources. I did some speculating, with advice Bill Gladwin gave me. I made money and I consider that mine. It will carry me."

Warren burst out, "You little fool! I meant to marry you."

Her head jerked up at him. Her eyes were amazed. "God help me, what kind of fool am I leaving?"

"If you'd had eyes you could have seen!"

"If I'd suspected—God! To think I was sleeping in the same house with you and you were lying in your bed planning this. If I'd known I might have—No, if you'd touched me. If you'd taken a step towards me I'd have killed you."

"Linda!"

"I'd as soon have married King Farouk!"

She went out and slammed the office door. She left behind her coat, her purse, and Warren.

Warren went back to his desk and sat heavily behind it. He bent his head for a minute and tried to keep from crying. Then, feverishly, he wrenched at his telephone. "Miss Johnson," he said crisply, "I've concluded the deal for the sale of the Kateena Mine. I want you to—"

His voice suddenly ceased. There was a great contraction in his throat, a complete block that would not let him speak or breathe. Slowly he replaced the telephone. He slumped back in his chair, exhaled slowly, and felt his throat loosen. Then he could breathe, but his breath came in deep, shaking dry sobs.

Scene Four

Into a low, well-upholstered cellar where women of distinction, and a few noticeably effeminate men, habitually ate lunch, strode Linda.

The place was called the Cabana. It was the lower floor of a good restaurant, the food was delectable, the cocktails good, and the decor tastefully Bohemian. Gossipy parties of women occupied some of the little tables, but the dim, cool atmosphere of the room hushed them to sibilant whisperers.

The head waiter came, graciously smiling, and Linda said, "Adolf, I'm broke. You'll have to cash a cheque for me."

"Of course, of course, Miss Warren."

"Well, bring me a blank cheque with my coffee, then. No, don't show me a table; I'll find one."

She went on through the room and paused suddenly at a table where a young woman was sitting alone.

"Hello, Nicole," she said loudly.

Nicole had been staring into her plate, rearranging the remains of her luncheon with a fork. She was startled as she looked up. "Oh—Linda! Hello."

"I suppose you know Charles is all right."

"I—I have no reason to worry about him. What do you mean?"

"The fire."

"Fire?"

"Oh, I'll sit with you, if you're not set on solitary thought." The waiter appeared and Linda said, "I want a Manhattan. No. A double Manhattan. And I want it this week."

"What do you mean about a fire?" Nicole asked.

"Charles is all right. Don't worry."

"Was Charles in a building which burnt?"

"He was in the gambling house. It burned down last night, but he left before the fire started."

"Was anyone hurt?"

"You haven't seen the morning paper."

"No."

"Bill Gladwin was trapped in the house. He died."

Tears came to Nicole's eyes. "Oh, poor Bill! I hope—"

"— he died quickly? Yes, I'm sure he did. The place was an inferno. He'd have no time to think or feel."

"There was no one else?"

"I almost went crazy all night, thinking Franz had been caught there too. I only found out an hour ago he was all right. Called his apartment—Marius answered. I was all ready to pass out, but he said Franz was not hurt. I suppose they were questioning him about the fire, since it was his house."

"His—I don't understand. Wait, you mean the gambling house belonged to Franz?"

"I thought you knew him better than that! Of course it did."

"Oh, no, no!"

"Why not? What's wrong with that? Or don't you like the idea that Franz was taking all Charles' money from him?"

"Ah, then that was what Charles meant," Nicole said slowly.

"By what?"

"Just—something he said. He was being ruined by his gambling? And it was Franz who"—her voice trailed away. She looked wildly around the room with a frightened, staring gaze; she brought her eyes back to Linda, but could not meet her look for more than an instant. She lowered her head. Then suddenly she stood up, rocking the tiny table, spilling a full glass of water. "Linda, I must go," she said in a panic.

"Sit down, you dam' idiot."

"Let me get out, get away. I can't break down and make a scene here."

"Sit down and stop working yourself up," Linda said firmly.

Nicole lowered herself to her seat and stared blankly at the white tablecloth. In no time Linda had summoned the waiter, had ordered a liqueur glass of cognac which was placed before Nicole.

"All right, drink it. No, damn it, don't sip!" Linda snapped. "Drink it in a gulp."

Nicole drank, and gasped. Her eyes slowly cleared and she seemed to relax.

"What was the trouble?" Linda asked.

"Oh, consider, Linda. Consider the number of shocks you passed to me in the space of a minute. That Charles is almost caught in a fire; that Bill is dead. That Charles has ruined himself gambling, that Franz—"

"Franz. That did it, didn't it?"

"It ranks with others as a shock."

"You in love with Franz?"

"You have no right to ask that."

"Oh, yes, I have. I'm in love with him myself."

"You?"

"Sure. And I'll tell you two things about it. First, this is the first love I've had that hasn't worn off in two weeks. Second, I hate being in love with him. And can I make a guess? I'll bet you're the same way exactly. You are in love with Franz. And you don't want to be in love with him."

"If I were in love with him, it would do me no good, of course. I'm married. For that reason you are right—I would not want to be in love with any man but Charles."

"Did you say that the wrong way, or can I take it you want to be in love with Charles—but aren't."

"Now you're being too curious again, Linda. That is not your concern."

"I suppose not. Let's get back to friends, though. I'm in love with Franz, like a fool. Franz is in love with you—of course he is," she added, as Nicole tossed her head doubtfully. "You're married, which completes the triangle. Or makes it a quadrangle, I don't know. Anyway—don't love Franz. Don't make a move toward him. He would never make a decent man for you, Nicole, no matter how much he loved you."

"I don't see why you say that," she said, puzzled.

"Listen to me. My heart's away out here in my hand, where I can watch it and everyone else can see it. Franz is my only love, because he's the only one I ever met tough enough to run me, and man enough to make me accept that. You know, if they're soft enough to break beneath me I throw them away. If they're too tough to break it's usually from ignorance or queerness. But Franz has got it, right on the line, for me. And he doesn't want me, so I hate myself for wanting him."

"He doesn't want you? Why?"

"I've told you. There's only one reason. He wants you. Maybe you're his mother-image, I don't know. But he wants you and if he gets you, it's the end of you, Nicole, don't forget that. I won't say he's too much of a man for you; I like you, and I don't think I could say that and mean it. But he's too tough for you. Too hard, self-centered, bull-headed, dictatorial. He'll break you, the way I broke all the other men."

Nicole shrugged and said with a little Gallic smile, "Perhaps he would break me and I would love that too."

"You think you would. But wait and see what it means. It means there's no *you* anymore. Beyond that it means, with the two of you, there's no *we*. There's only Franz. No, he needs a foil. He needs a woman like me as I need a man like him. And yet he wants you, and you probably want him, and so in the end I suppose another of life's great mistakes will be made. God—life!"

"Linda, I must go," said Nicole, and before Linda, who sat brooding over her own last words, could protest, she had gone.

She hailed a taxi outside the Cabana and said, "the Frontenac Apartments, please."

And leaning quietly back in the seat of the taxi, trying so hard to again become calm, she thought.

That Charles had almost died. That Charles was ruined. That Bill Gladwin was dead. That Franz had ruined Charles. That Franz loved her. That Linda wanted her to stay away from Franz. That...

Oh, God, God, what was important?

Was all her life and past and whatever that meant important, or was it only important that she loved Franz and he loved her?

She loved Franz? How could she possibly love a man she did not know? A man she had not known to be a gambler, a criminal! A man who, without her knowing had, in the guise of friendship, taken everything from Charles—Charles, of whom she could think many things, but whom she could never hate.

What was this man?

He could not have become a gambler only for money and position, to delude his friends and take things from them. He could not have set out to ruin Charles simply because he thought it would bring me to him. He is not that man.

He had other reasons for doing what he has done. I will know them when I talk to him. He's been trying to do something, something not as evil as this seems—and he has failed. If it is true that Charles is ruined, it is at least certainly true that Franz himself has fallen. His gambling house is gone, and everyone must know he is a gambler. His friends will no longer be friends—and the best of his friends, Bill Gladwin, is dead. It is clear. He must leave Montreal.

And I shall go with him!

Oh, what does it matter how Linda talked. She doesn't know.

He has only to explain, to tell me why he did these things and I will be his.

She bit her lips, and her eyes narrowed. Into this head-long rush of thought her minded interjected one word: Madness!

Her taxi drew up the circling drive of the Frontenac, stopped, and the driver opened her door. As she paid him, as she walked slowly into the building and waited for the elevator to come to her, the thoughts ran on.

I am being only a hedonist, she acknowledged fully. I am going in search of pleasure, love, happiness I cannot possibly find with Charles. I am leaving everything to start a new, better life—only to satisfy myself. Can I justify the hurt I will do Charles and my family and everyone here by the goodness of this new life?

Will it be truly good—*truly good*, though a priest condemn it—or will it just be satisfaction of my desires?

It seemed to her honestly that it would be good, truly good, not only for her but for Franz, because of the things she could do for him. He was a hurt and bitter man, one deeply unsure of life and himself despite his surface hardness. And then, through her, the things Franz could do for people, for the world, would be good. They would have done these things together. It could not be as Linda believed.

I am willing to throw away my small hope of paradise, she thought, for something truly good as this.

And again she thought, there's been some reason for the way Franz has behaved. There's been something behind this superficial wickedness, for Franz could be cruel and mistaken and selfish—but he could not be evil. He only has to tell me.

And if he tells me, I shall go with him.

She was completely sure of herself.

She entered the elevator and rode to the top of the building.

At the penthouse door, she pressed the bell.

Scene Five

It was very early in the day for Charles to be this drunk.

He pressed the starter button on the car. Nothing happened. He pressed again.

He squinted blearily down to the instrument panel, saw what was wrong, grunted in annoyance, turned the ignition key, and started the car.

He had been parked in the driveway just opposite the Frontenac. He roared out from the driveway and made a lurching turn down Côte des Neiges Road, into a full stream of traffic; brakes locked, tires squealed and a few horns bayed behind him. But he was launched into the stream, and he continued at a quite illegal pace until he reached Sherbrooke Street where, making an illegal left-hand turn, he went east until he came to a large and exclusive hotel. Leaving his car at the side of the street to invite a parking ticket, he made his way to the hotel's downstairs bar. It was a small room and, at this time of the afternoon, deserted. Charles sat at the bar and beckoned the bartender.

"George. George, want one of those tall, thin, maroon-coloured drinks of yours. What you call 'em? Brown bombers."

George sized up the state of Charles' being and said, very pleasantly, "Sorry, Mr. Porter-Smythe. We don't serve those drinks this time of day. Those are strictly evening drinks."

"Oh, c'mon, don't be silly. You got a time lock on your mixing memory? Make me one."

"No, sir, Mr. Porter-Smythe, not unless you want to go to sleep right here. Those drinks are bad medicine, this early. Anyway I think you've had a few now, haven't you?"

"George, I got a sad task ahead of me. I need a brown bomber. Don' worry, I can handle it. You ever had to carry me out of here?"

"No, sir," George lied.

"Well, I'll tell you this sad story. You a dog man?"

"Yes, sir. I love dogs."

"I've got a dog. Dog I love. But he's sick." Charles took a small automatic out of his jacket pocket and looked at it meditatively. He waved it at George. "'S all right, it's loaded. But I know it. The safety's on. You know what I've got to do, George? You can guess. Got to shoot that poor dog."

"Ah, that's a shame."

Charles put his gun carefully back in his jacket pocket. "Well, do I get my brown bomber? Got to have this one more drink and then I'll do this sad job."

"One brown bomber coming up, sir."

Scene Six

"Nicole!" Franz said.

Her face held what was for him a beautiful anxiety, a questioning. She had never seemed more alive. He watched her an instant and knew somehow that she was his, that she had changed fundamentally so that he could take her for his own.

He said, "Come in. We will sit here."

"You must tell me everything. About the gambling house and what you have been doing."

"It is quickly told. A friend, Morrie Winter, owned the gambling house on LaGarde Street. He died, and it was his wish I operate the house. I decided to do so."

"Why, Franz?"

"So the house would not fall into the hands of the man who killed my friend."

"That was all?"

"No. I wanted the house as a weapon against the man. Through it I wanted to obtain the wealth and then the power to overthrow him."

"And it was worthwhile to deceive your friends, perhaps ruin them, for this purpose?"

"Yes."

"Was there no other way?"

"The man had been a clever fiend; the murder of

Winter could not be proved. Even a stupid murder could not be used to convict this man, for he owns too large a part of Montreal. I had to match his power, to defeat him—unless I wished simply to assassinate, to execute him."

"Who is this man?"

"Rosaire Beaumage."

"Yes, I know him. I know his name. But you must tell me—was it only for revenge you became a gambler?"

"Revenge? I did not think so much of revenge as of the need to rid Montreal of this evil."

"I believe that too. And the other reasons?"

"I cannot deny that I needed the money and wanted the power I was building for myself. They allowed me to live as I had been accustomed to live. I thought, too, that they brought me closer to you."

"These were secondary things."

"Nicole, nothing connected with you could be a secondary thing. But the link between you and the gambling was secondary."

"Oh, I am glad! All you have said makes me glad."

"But there's more. The death of Bill Gladwin, and the effect on Charles—"

"I know. Franz, you said you loved me."

"I can love no one else."

"And I love you."

Franz stood. "I know that," he said quietly. "I know that we love each other, and I know also you have decided we can do nothing with that love. How have you changed?"

"I will go away with you."

She stood also, and they held each other at arms' length.

"I have left the past," she went on, "feeling that it matters as little as though it had happened in another incarnation. Of those we leave behind, we can think only that it will be better for them when we have gone. Everything is finished now for us here, and we can go away together and enter a new world."

"Nicole, Nicole, I cannot go."

"What do you mean? It is finished. The house is burnt, your friends are lost, Gladwin is dead..."

"Rosaire Beaumage is not dead."

"Then what can you do to him? Your power to defeat him has been dissolved. You could only assassinate him."

"Now I must do that."

"But that is simply murder. You cannot fight that way."

"Cannot fight evil with evil? That is what I have been doing, Nicole, but in the wrong way. The way I fought meant safety, even luxury for me—and death for others. Now I will kill Rosaire, and place only my own life in jeopardy."

"No, no, you cannot! You love me. We cannot consummate that love unless we go—go today, away from Montreal."

"I cannot go. With all my love for you, I cannot go. If I were to leave, and leave behind me Rosaire, it would all have been worthless."

They held each other still at arms' length. The doorbell rang.

Scene Seven

"Hello," Charles said. "Came to get my wife."

Franz stood directly in front of the open door, blocking him.

"I'm coming in, you know," Charles said mildly. He pawed awkwardly in his pocket and came out with the automatic. He released the safety catch. "Please," he said.

Franz backed carefully away from the door. Charles was drunk, and his manner might hide any kind of feeling.

"Nicole!" Charles called, catching sight of the girl. "Come here, Nicole. Want to talk to you both for a minute, if you don't mind."

She crossed the room very slowly and placed herself beside Franz. "Charles, please," she said. "Charles."

"I have to say this, my dear. I'm sorry. Franz, we have a lot in common. Both lost a good friend in that fire. Both lost our businesses last night. I lost mine to you. You lost yours to Rosaire. Winslow got mine and passed it on for what it was worth to him. Passed it on to C.C. Warren. Very cold-blooded, isn't it, talking business at a time like this. No, not so cold-blooded. Emotion in it too. I liked you, Franz, I did like you. I wanted you to help me, with my business. I wanted you to run it for me because I trusted you and I liked you. You were the only man I ever asked for help like that. You wouldn't help me, but I didn't think you'd bleed me to death."

Charles raised the hand holding the gun to his eyes, and used the back of his hand to rub once across his forehead, as though trying to clear his vision. Franz steeled himself to jump, but Charles brought the gun down and levelled it again. Franz thought: when he does that again...

"And then Nicole," Charles said. "I don't know whose fault it is. Your fault. Hers. Mine. Don't know. But I wouldn't have believed it. I had to see it. I see it."

He paused, looking steadily at Franz. "There's nothing else I can do, Franz," he said, and his finger tensed on the trigger.

"No!" Nicole screamed, and threw herself before Franz.

The gun's noise exploded. Nicole's hands flailed, and closed over her breast; she sank back heavily against Franz, but with her eyes still wide and staring, seeing Charles look at her in incredulous horror, then turn the gun to his own head and shoot again.

Scene Eight

Wally Burns was fully dressed, from dog-eared shoes to drooping fedora; he had left on his voluminous coat because his flat was none too warm. He plodded through his dilapidated quarters, sloshing beer glass in one hand, foaming beer quart in the other. As he reached his front door, knuckles again rattled upon it.

Wally said, "Cathy, I'm undressed an' in bed. Go 'way an' I'll see you tomorrow."

"It's Franz Loebek, Burns."

"Hah? Oh." Wally transferred the glass to the hand holding the quart, not spilling much of the beer. He twisted the spring lock. "Come on in."

Franz entered and doffed his hat.

Wally said, "Yes, I'm a solitary drinker. Always solitary drink when I try to write stories. Damnedest profession in the world, writing stories. Take detective stories. Try to keep the reader from solvin' the plot. What if you can't solve it yourself? You know, I've been working on this thing—"

"I don't know whether I may ask you a favour."

"I don' know either. What is it?"

"About—keeping something out of the papers. I do not know how it is done, or whether it can be done."

"I don't keep things out of papers," Burns said belligerently, "I put things in. Whose good name we trying to save now?"

"Not mine, though this occurred at my apartment. A shooting."

"Who's shot?"

"Charles and Nicole Porter-Smythe."

"My God, both?"

Franz nodded.

"Who shot them?"

"Charles."

"Oh, fine. Then what happened?"

"Ambulances. Police. There will be a report, of course."

Wally wiped his mouth thoughtfully with the back of his hand. "Yeah, sure. But with a name like Porter-Smythe, I don't think you have to worry. Worst thing that could happen is a small, buried item saying a man had shot his wife and himself in an apartment on Côte des Neiges. No names."

"You are quite sure?"

"I c'n make some phone calls and *be* sure. I'll see there's no one in the slot dumb enough to shove it through. Sit down an' wait."

"Thanks. I am reassured. I have much to do. I appreciate that greatly."

"I'm not quite sure who I'm doing it for. I'm not sure I'm doing it for you. But that's okay, anyway."

"Good night."

Franz stepped through the doorway from Wally's flat to a wide porch that fronted the building. The little side street was dimly lit, and snow from the last fall had not yet been properly removed; it stood about in great piles, frosted with the black from city chimneys. Across the street, Jules Trebonne had parked Cab 613 and was waiting for Franz.

He started down the steps, and at that instant saw a long, black limousine come slowly down the street toward him.

Franz stopped, immobile, and then slowly shrank back into the shadows at the side of the porch. He crouched below the lighted window through which could be seen Wally, now returned to his typewriter and his beer. The limousine stopped directly in front of the door. Franz retreated to the very corner of the porch; reaching deep into his heavy overcoat, he brought out an old military revolver of heavy calibre.

From the limousine came Rosaire, Jean-Paul and a third man. They came quickly up the steps and held a brief conference in French beside the door of Wally's flat.

"There he is," Rosaire said. "Observe, through this front window. Jean-Paul, when you use your key on the door I will go in very quietly and go to that room. I will be in plain view at all times. You will watch, and if anything

190

goes wrong you will come immediately. Come through the window if you must, but avoid shooting through the window."

"Correct," Jean-Paul replied. "Be sure to stay where we can see you." He went to the door and unlocked it silently in a few seconds with the skeleton key.

Rosaire stole into the flat; he closed the door behind him, but it did not latch.

Franz was placed where he could not see through the lighted window, but very shortly he heard Jean-Paul whisper to his companion, "*Voilà*, he is there. Be ready."

Inside, Wally paused in his typing as a shadow fell across his work. He looked up.

"Good evening, Mr. Burns," Rosaire greeted him.

"Well. Well. Monsieur Beaumage. This is a real unusual honor. What d' you want?"

"A little chat, Mr. Burns. A rather unpleasant little chat. Today I received a sheaf of proof-sheets. They were the proofs of a story to be published in some cheap English magazine. A most ingenious little story."

"Of course."

"I think you know the plot of this little tale, Burns, but I shall tell it to you. It concerns the murder of a man by poison, a murder subtly done with an obscure chemical so that it appeared the man had died of cancer."

"Spare me the details."

"Undoubtedly you wrote the story?"

"Perhaps I did. Perhaps I only heard the theory of the way Morrie Winter died."

"In this story justice, of course, triumphs. A wise-cracking detective discovers how the crime was committed and traps a murderer into a confession. I do not like that ending."

"Come, Beaumage, isn't it the right one?"

"Of course. But I do not like it if the finger points to me. What else could be the implication, when I am sent the proofs of the story? What is your purpose, Burns; blackmail?"

Wally laughed. "Perhaps just curiosity. Perhaps now that curiosity has been satisfied."

"Ah, to what dangers a curious person exposes himself. My dear Burns, we must have a very long talk. This is a poor place to talk. Come"—he extended his hand—"finish your glass, and we will go."

Wally got to his feet in a hurry, knocking his chair over backward. "You stupid bastard, I saw that! A little dusting of silver powder in my beer. What did you put in my beer?"

Outside the window Jean-Paul said to the other, "They're starting to quarrel. I do not like this. Come, we'll go in."

"Gentlemen." Franz spoke sharply from his corner, in French. "Hold up your hands, and turn your backs to the window. Quickly! I will not hesitate to shoot."

The men obeyed but kept a safe distance from him. He said, "Please do not make a foolish move. I can see you perfectly in the light from the window. There's already been too much killing. Now, go toward your automobile."

As they turned to go down the steps, Jean-Paul stole one glance at the window. The two inside were still standing, facing each other, talking loudly but not moving. He could only pray, for his sake as much as for Rosaire's, that his chief was safe.

They approached the big limousine and Jules Trebonne, who had been waiting and watching quietly, emerged beside them.

"Take their weapons, Jules," Franz directed him. "Very carefully; do not obstruct my line of fire... Fine. Now open the car door for them."

The men climbed unprotestingly into the limousine. "Goodbye, gentlemen," Franz said. "Don't come back for at least an hour. We will be waiting for you until then."

Inside Wally's flat, after the men had left the window, the scene between Rosaire and Wally had been played on.

"What's in my beer?" Wally repeated. "Trying to poison me too?"

"Drink your beer and you will sleep, Burns. When you are awake we will talk. Drink, it is the only thing to do."

Wally came around the table toward Rosaire. "Just a sleeping potion, is it? You know what? I'm going to let you drink it instead."

"Keep back! Two of my men are waiting just there, at the window. You invite death."

"I'll take my chances."

He leapt at Rosaire, bearing him to the floor beneath him. Rosaire shrank into himself, closing his eyes, waiting for the heavy roar of a gun. Nothing happened. He opened his eyes and stared wildly at the window, at the door of the room. No one burst in to rescue him. "Jean-Paul!" he screamed.

Burns bashed his head back against the floor to quiet him, and sat up, astride his prone body. Rosaire's arms were pinned under two chunky knees and he twisted vainly trying to escape from the solid bulk above him.

"Now, we'll see how good this medicine is," Wally grinned. He reached carefully to the table, grabbed his beer glass, and brought it down into position over Rosaire's mouth. With the thumb and forefinger of his other hand, he squeezed shut Rosaire's nostrils.

Rosaire screamed. Wally waited patiently and when the scream was quite through, at Rosaire's gasping inhalation of breath, into his gaping mouth, poured a generous portion of beer. Rosaire gagged and swallowed unwillingly, and then seemed to give up his struggle. Each time he gasped for breath again, he received a little more beer.

When the beer glass was more than half empty, Rosaire twisted his body with a great convulsion, and sobbed. He upset neither Burns nor the beer. His voice was weak as he cried, "Wait! My God, wait!" Burns waited—until the sentence was done and Rosaire had to breathe again. Then he poured in more beer.

As Franz rushed into the room, Wally was emptying the glass into Rosaire's mouth. Rosaire's eyes had glazed over, and his body was quite still. Wally crouched forward, ready to spring on the newcomer, until he recognized Franz.

"Are you all right? I heard the scream, but was busy."

"Oh, you take care of the gorillas? Rosaire was advertisin' he had a couple planted outside. Thanks."

"Who gave the scream?"

Wally rolled off Rosaire and lurched to his feet. "Not me." He looked complacently down at Rosaire. "Well, I wonder what that will do to him? Interesting to see."

"What did you do?"

"Fed him the Mickey Finn he fixed for me."

Franz bent over Rosaire and looked at him keenly. Rosaire's eyes were open and staring. He could see. He could not speak.

Wally said, "He claimed this was a little medicine to put me to sleep for a while. Let's see how it puts him to sleep."

"My God, I wonder if—" Franz knelt beside Rosaire. He ripped the man's jacket aside and felt for the heartbeat. Then he stood up slowly again.

"Yes, that is it," he said. "He is dying. It is the poison he used to kill Willie Cameron."

"My lucky day," Wally grunted. He watched Rosaire. "Seems to be having trouble with his breathing."

"He won't breathe much longer."

"Well, well. Wait till I get two clean glasses and another quart, and we can drink to that."

"No. I will not celebrate. *You* killed him. *You* killed him," Franz repeated. "Now all I have done, all the wrong I have done, all has been worthless."

EIGHT

Scene One

The room was like all hospital rooms, no better, no worse. A small attempt had been made to brighten it with flowered chintz curtains, matching the flowered chintz of the screen that hid the lavatory. The walls were pastel rather than glaring white. But the floor was dark, hard and antiseptically bare; the great high hulk of the Hatch bed made the rest of the furniture in the room look squat.

Franz, having checked with the special nurse, knocked quietly and came into the room. Nicole was almost sitting in the bed, supported by the cranked-up spring. Only her head sagged backward, and her eyes were just half-open. Her hair been caught back under a plain white linen band and her face was colourless and wan. She said tonelessly, "Franz. I've waited for you. It has been so terrible."

"The pain?"

"No, I am comfortable. They operated this morning to take out the bullet, but it was a short operation. The shoulder pains sometimes, but they have been generous with their drugs."

"What is the trouble?"

"Charles, and you, and I."

"No, you must not talk. I must talk. I must tell you all I have thought of in the long, long time since this happened.

"Now we are free, but we are not free. I have thought that over and over, and always it is the same. You see, it was so nearly right last night that we should go away together. Only Rosaire stood between us, and he could not have been there forever."

195

Franz said, "And now Rosaire is dead."

"Dead? I do not even care how he died. But that is great irony, is it not? Last night he alone held us apart. Now everything holds us apart."

"Yes. Many things."

"Perhaps it would never have worked out. Perhaps it was only the belief of a minute of craziness. But I thought we could leave behind all that had happened here, everyone who was entangled with our life here, and start again and build something fine together."

"Do you believe we could have done that, when we were in flight from all the things we had known?"

"I see that you could not have fled from Rosaire, and left the field to him; but you had nothing else to leave behind. And me, I had no debts, no unpaid bills to leave here if I went away with you. We were leaving nothing, in comparison with what we were taking away from Montreal—the only worthwhile thing for us—our love for each other. And it was a good love."

"*Was* it a good love?"

"It was a good love until last night. Then it killed Charles, and became in an instant an evil love. There were the germs of evil in it, all the time. It was an illicit, unblest love; but it was too great to be restricted by that. When Charles acted, he destroyed the good in our love."

"You say it had a germ of evil, Nicole. Can any such love be good? Our love denied the rights of anyone else. I wanted you, I cared for nothing else. I would have taken you from anyone, anything, had you been willing to come with me. Then you were willing, and—all that we had denied and neglected exploded on us, when Charles fired his gun."

"Yes. That is what I thought. I know now that we must always be apart, that we can never see each other again, even though Charles is dead. If he had died in any other way not God nor man could have held us apart. But now—"

"Even had he not died, we would have to part now."

"Yes, you are right. What has happened was the judgement on our love. Nothing else that you had done, or that I had done, could have defeated it."

"Nicole, they have not told you because you did not dare to ask. I will tell you. Charles is not dead."

"Charles—" her eyes widened and she pushed herself forward in the bed. "But I saw! My God, my Lord, before I was unconscious I saw him shoot—"

"He was too drunk, luckily, to shoot straight—even in shooting himself. The bullet tore his scalp and grazed his skull. He is not even in danger."

"And he is—"

"In another room of this hospital."

"Oh, thank God. I considered myself the only cause of his death. Thank God!"

"I hope only one thing now. I'm going away, Nicole. Perhaps you and Charles would have become more happy, instead of farther apart, had I not been here. Once I have gone you can try again to make a marriage. Slowly—"

"But there will always be our love!"

"Our love. Our great love, the love that made you throw yourself before me, to take the bullet meant for me. There can be no love like that, Nicole. But you will change, now, and Charles will change. There can be a marriage full of happiness without our kind of love, Nicole. Our kind— it is a love few know. It is a love some tortured ones, like us, are shown but briefly before it is torn away. Most people must live without it, without even having thought of it. Knowing it, and thankful to have known it, we can still build our lives."

"But Charles; can Charles change?"

"After the crisis of last night no one could be unchanged. You can only hope. But I predict—you will see."

"And what of you, Franz?"

"I found a new employment. I shall fly again, but not as I flew before, a hunter and killer. I have fought my fight against the evil in humans, and found I am not the man

197

to do that. I fought evil men with evil. I did not defeat the enemy, but did great wrong in my attempt. There are other things than men to fight against."

"What things?"

"The wasteland, the bitter north. I am going far into the north now."

"And you will be happy?"

He shrugged. "I will have something to do. That is important. Now I must go."

He turned at the door and said, "Goodbye, Nicole. I will go quickly."

The door closed behind him. Nicole shut her eyes, and after a time she slept.

Scene Two

Linda made a phone call from a hotel booth.

"Warren," came the voice on the line.

"Hello, Father. Don't hang up or you'll be sorry."

Warren said unpleasantly, "I have no great desire to have you call me Father. And you can stop calling yourself Warren. Your legal name is Scittanelli."

"Doesn't matter a bit. I'm going to change it soon, anyway. Listen, *Father*, this is blackmail."

"I might have expected something of the sort, I suppose."

"Not for me. I'll never take another share of General Motors stock from you. This is another matter."

"Well?"

"I want to remind you of a few little things. Remember the plan to control the frozen peas pack this summer? Depends pretty heavily on secrecy, doesn't it? And that business of the Penshore Gold manipulation—the stocks would fall considerably in value if the market found your geologist was talking about the one good drill core, not the ten bad ones—wouldn't they? And the matter of the—"

"All right, that's enough. It's quite plain what you're threatening to do. What do you want?"

"You just do this. You take no more than ten percent interest in Charles Porter-Smythe's business in exchange for that note of his you hold. Understand?"

There was silence from the other end of the line.

"All right, you heard me," Linda said grimly. "And I'll find out fast enough, if you try to pull anything else." She hung up.

Scene Three

Wally said, "What did you mean—'It was all worthless?' That was a nice exit line, but it didn't stack up. All you were trying to do all the time, to hear you tell the story, was wipe out Rosaire. Okay, he's wiped out. Why be so disconsolate?"

Franz crossed the great master bedroom of his Frontenac penthouse with his arms full of clothes from the closet. He threw them on the bed and began methodically folding them into a suitcase. "Why are you here now?" he asked Wally. "More story? More detail? A new angle?"

"No, I'm working on my own time this afternoon. Freelance. I'm just studying you. I may want to write a novel about you sometime."

"Oh. I see."

"For God's sake, come on. Snap out of it. Don't you know who your friends are yet? I'm not trying to pump you for a story. I'm interested, and if you don't believe that, I'll go."

"Sorry. Do not go. Sometimes I labour under the delusion that I have no friends."

"It's a serious defect in your personality. Why are you leaving Montreal?"

"Why should I stay?"

"Why not take over Rosaire's empire, and run it honestly?"

"No. I could not do that. It is not what I want—though I suppose I was heading in that direction, if I had fully faced the facts. But I wanted more than that—and less. I had landed between the two mountains."

"What do you mean?"

"Nicole—Nicole Porter-Smythe—first said it. You observe this building, this penthouse: the high windows look out on the city. But the foundations of the building are between the two mountains. Neither in the social hill of Westmount, nor in the business hill of Montreal, but pressing rudely up between both to reach their height.

"I was the same. I was neither all business, as the successor of Rosaire must be—a needed cog in a well-running society. Nor was I content to be just social, a well-paid aristocrat in a position that amounted to a sinecure. I had to try for the best of both worlds, both mountains. The prestige of the wealthy man of leisure. The power of the scheming businessman. Well—I fell between the mountains."

"You fell. You can get up and change your suit, can't you?"

"No. I have been wrong in all my methods. I do not trust myself to start again in anything like the same situation. You see, I set myself to right a wrong in my own way. That involved the breaking of laws to catch a criminal. I was not successful. I could not be ruthless enough to shoot Rosaire in cold blood and become entirely an outlaw myself, as I should have done. I wanted to crush him by his own means—destroy evil, yes—but gain power as I did it. Well, you've seen what happened. Rosaire killed Winter. I'm at least partially responsible for the deaths of Gladwin, of Willie Cameron."

"Only partly."

"That is enough. No, I can only acknowledge myself a sinner and do penance, now. There are emergencies such as war, where one uses the means at hand to defeat the enemy. I made a false analogy. I declared my own private war against Rosaire, and fought him as I had fought the Boche. But one does not use such means in an ordered society. It can only mean chaos. I thought I was above the law, that I would work against the law to trap a mad dog. Instead, I caught the hydrophobia."

"No more vigilante work, eh?"

"No. The wretchedness of my failure was complete when I saw Rosaire die from your poison drink—"

"*His* poison drink."

"The poison drink you fed him. That is a small thing to quibble over. The fact is that almost by chance, you disposed of him. I had schemed and fought and laboured, and he had used his own methods more effectively than I. I was defeated, and even had I killed him myself, there was no real victory for me. I had not in the end even the sacrifice of offering myself in exchange for him, to rid the place of us both."

"Your society venture didn't turn out too well either, did it?"

"You mean Nicole? There again I tried to place myself above the law—this time, the law of the Church. No, I have thought myself too great a man. It is well to think of oneself as great in mastery over things, over ideas. But a great man is not the master and dictator of others. He cannot be more than their leader, to be great."

"You going somewhere and lead people?"

Franz laughed. "No. I'm going away to master some things. Some very intractable and rebellious things, Burns. The wilds. I've found a job as a bush-pilot. I'm away for the northwest; first stop, after I've gathered up my kit, Edmonton."

"When do you leave Montreal?"

"Bill Gladwin's funeral is this afternoon. Then I go."

"I ever get out that way, I'll look you up. Wish we got to know each other sooner. No, maybe I don't. Maybe I wouldn't have liked you before. Seems as if you've changed. There's something in this process of living and learning, isn't there?" Burns stopped and scratched his head. "Remind me, I wonder what I've learned lately?"

"How to kill fiends," Franz said grimly.

"No, that's not fair. I only killed him because I was too drunk to be scared, and drunk enough to lose my temper. See what that teaches me? Nothing good."

"And what have I learned?" Franz mused.

"Let me try to put it in words. I'm supposed to have words for things. You've learned your own limitations, or perhaps I should say, the limitations of any individual under law—to fight evil only as a citizen, wading through the red tape if you have to. You've learned the usefulness of organized society, no matter how disorganized it sometimes seems. In a word, yes, a single word—you've been civilized, Franz."

"I think you are right. Well, I am packed. Let us leave this unlucky place. Marius has already gone."

"Where?"

"To Toronto. He got the staff of the gambling house from there. He's going back with them."

As they waited for the elevator together Franz said, "I am leaving a lot of money here. Think, and later tell me to whom I should give it. I will write to give you my address."

"Okay. Be sure to write," Burns said. "I want to know where to send the novel when I get it published."

Scene Four

Warren paused at the door of the room, and did his best to manage a smile. He said cheerfully "That's a very distinguished looking bandage you're wearing, Charles."

"Come in, Colonel, come in," Charles said gaily. "I'm glad the bandage looks important. They've shaved off half my hair, and I'll have to wear it for months."

"How are you feeling, my boy?"

"Colonel, I haven't felt better in years. Do you know, this makes the second day I haven't had a drop of alcohol?

I never realized how wonderful life was, without it. I started to drink so young that I can't remember not drinking. Now I'm planning to join the A.A.—not because I have to, you understand. Because I may be able to do some good with it."

"Charles, I have something to say. Are you well enough to discuss business?"

"I told you I've never felt better."

"After all that's happened, I admit I'm ashamed of myself. I was harsh and unchristian with you, about your business. I didn't realize quite how much it meant to you, I guess. Now, I want to make a really generous agreement with you. I'll gladly exchange your note for a ten percent share in the firm."

"How much would you like to pay for another forty-one percent?"

"You—wait, I don't follow you, Charles. You mean you're willing to give me control of your business?"

"At a fair price, yes."

"I thought that was the very thing you were frantically determined to prevent."

"That was two days ago, Colonel. I've had a little time to think. First consecutive two-day period I've ever spent thinking without the aid of rye whisky. Now, the main conclusion I've come to is the one you tried to impress on me in your office. I'm just not a businessman. No sense wasting my life and ruining my disposition trying to be one, merely because my father was a small-scale robber baron. So I'm going to let you have my business—gladly, if we can agree on terms. After all, Colonel, no matter what I think of your manipulations, you're an eminently successful businessman. And I intend to vote my stock and live handsomely on the dividends you'll produce from Porter Bolt and Screw."

"Well, we can certainly talk this over. As soon as you're up and about. I hope I've helped clear up some of your worries, though, by coming here."

"I wasn't worried about the business. I have one very grave worry, but aside from that I'm bursting to get out of here. Have a lot of things to do that I never had time for before. Charity work. Community work. Why, I might even run for mayor of Westmount in a few years!"

"That sounds wonderful, Charles. I think you're making a wise decision. And I know we'll do well as partners."

"Thanks, Colonel, I'm sure we will. Now, if you'll excuse me, someone else is waiting outside to see me."

Warren orated a few more pleasantries and went out beaming. A moment later, a priest entered the room.

"Father. I've been waiting anxiously to see you."

"And I to see you. Are you better?"

"I'm almost well, Father, but I'm troubled. I'll make no bones about it. I'm in here because I shot my wife and then shot myself. Tried to kill myself. I intended to shoot a man, rather than my wife, but that doesn't make things better."

"And of all this, you repent?"

"I only hope repentance will be enough. I don't know what has happened between my wife and the other man, since the shooting. It could have drawn them together, and I can't blame Nicole for anything she wishes to do, now. But if there's any chance for a reconciliation, I'll fight for it with all my strength."

"What do you want me to do?"

"Will you go to her? Tell her that we have everything needed, everything in our favour, if we can only forget the past. Tell her I love her more than before we were married, more than I've ever loved her. Tell her, and I'm sure—I'm convinced..."

Scene Five

Linda said over the telephone, "I want to speak to one of your drivers. Number six-thirteen. I think his name is Julius Trebonne."

"It is Jules Trebonne. He is in a cab, madame. Maybe anywhere in the city."

"It's a radio cab, isn't it? Radio him and tell him to come pick me up here. At the Chatham Hotel. I'll watch for him."

"He may be all the way across the city. He would lose fares coming a long distance to get you."

"Dammit, man, I don't care if he's all the way across the St. Lawrence River. I want to talk to him. He'll be well rewarded. Tell him to come pick me up. Say Wally Burns gave me his name. No, say I'm a friend of Franz Loebek."

Scene Six

The man who had been an aristocrat, and then a hero, and then a gambler, sat in the bar room of a small Toronto hotel. He held his drained glass in his hands and in a habitual gesture, twirled it and stared into it. He saw in it a vista of frozen tundra, windswept lakes and black-green forest.

Franz had stopped in Toronto to check at the office of his bush airline employers, to assemble his flying kit, and to pick up a plane and ferry it to Edmonton. He had gravitated naturally to the Chiltern Hotel his first day; it was small and quiet. Its bar was very small, like some of the little bars in London. Comfortable, deeply carpeted to silence the waiters' flitting feet, dimly lit with no sharp glare. It was a good place to be.

The last stop in civilization, he thought idly, of Loebek, the newly civilized man.

What have I learned? To be civilized. And it has taken Canadians to teach me, when I come from the oldest civilized continent. Perhaps we are not truly civilized there...

The door to the bar room was pushed open suddenly, and emitted an indignant squawk. All heads turned to the door, and the woman who stood there, who intended to make this entrance, looked proudly about her.

She was a proud woman, with an insolent figure, the carriage of a princess and a face that would turn away from no one. She wore a strapless cocktail gown, jet-black, so beautifully fitted with its tight bodice that she might have been wrapped in latex. She had long golden hair.

She looked about the room, and then as she came towards Franz' table he stood and pulled out a chair for her.

"You're a hell of a man to locate. I almost had to break Jules Trebonne's arm."

"How did he know where I'd gone? I meant no one to know, for a while."

"He knew what time he'd driven you to the airport. I had an airline schedule. Don't underestimate me... I've sent my bags up to your room. Told them we are man and..."

"It's a little late. I can hardly marry you tonight."

"We're a bit beyond that already, aren't we? Anyway, I don't care. Don't marry me if you don't want to."

"I think I should not. Oh, do not think I fail to welcome you. But we will quarrel. One of us will leave the other."

"We'll quarrel beautifully. And if I leave you, I'll come back. If you leave me, I'll find you."

"You will not like where we are going."

"Where?"

"The wilderness. No cocktail parties. No bars. No good restaurants, no theatres, no heat, no bathrooms, and sometimes damned little food."

"I'll try it. I'm just ripe for a change. I threw up my Montreal life because I hated it, not because of you. I'd already sawed off the limb before I saw my chance to do this."

"All right. You can come and try it."

"Thanks. I was coming. I was prepared to try Edmonton if I missed you here."

She drained the drink he ordered for her, and stood. "That's enough drinking. Let's go to bed."

"Sit down."

"Come on."

206

"Sit down. We are each having one more drink."

Linda sat. She glared at him for a minute, but then thought of something else. She broke into a laugh.

"What is it?"

"I just remembered. You'd better marry me, after all, unless you want a girl named Scittanelli kicking around."

THE END

www.vehiculepress.com